In Caddis Wood

IN CADDIS WOOD

A Novel

To Julie & Maury —

" Be earth now, and evensong. "
Rilke

MARY FRANÇOIS ROCKCASTLE

Let's be sure to do more together. Lots of love —

Mary

Graywolf Press

This publication is made possible by funding provided in part by a grant from the Minnesota State Arts Board, through an appropriation by the Minnesota State Legislature, a grant from the National Endowment for the Arts, and private funders. Significant support has also been provided by Target; the McKnight Foundation; and other generous contributions from foundations, corporations, and individuals. To these organizations and individuals we offer our heartfelt thanks.

Special funding for this title has been provided by the Jerome Foundation.

Published by Graywolf Press
250 Third Avenue North, Suite 600
Minneapolis, Minnesota 55401

www.graywolfpress.org

Published in the United States of America

ISBN 978-1-55597-592-0

2 4 6 8 9 7 5 3 1
First Graywolf Printing, 2011

Library of Congress Control Number: 2011930480

Cover design: Christa Schoenbrodt, Studio Haus

Cover art: Regan Golden, *The Interior of a Forest*, 2010

For Garth

In Caddis Wood

CARL

Chapter 1

Caddis Wood (Early June)

Carl sits upright in bed and gazes into the furry dark. Something hot and galloping in the room, black walls leaping like a Tilt-A-Whirl, the steady thump of his heart. Terror. Not from a dream, either. Hallie sighs and turns into his arm. There is a stirring in the corner behind the glass door, and he remembers a similar movement that afternoon while he was weeding in the garden. A motion as of a bird startled, jarred into flight. Scanning the shadowy contours of the room, he sees the pale curtain, the silhouette of clothing hung on hooks. He concentrates on each breath, his eyes locked on the steepled pines that frame the edge of the porch, then pads across the wooden floor.

The air outside is resinous, soft, completely still. Only the silver stream moves. Maybe it's the unnatural quiet that has awakened him, the absence of nighttime's customary clamor: leaves, the soughing wind, whine of insects. The moon is sickle shaped and bright, not a single cloud. Everything—trees, sky, birds—is watching.

Without warning, the image of his own death comes upon him. Nothing concrete—no yellow car, no fire, no empty stairs. But the idea of it is so real he trembles. Look around, he counsels himself: the motionless meadow, the meandering hedgerows and flowery stream banks, the circular vegetable garden. This screened porch he's standing on, the wooden ledge beneath his hand. I made this place. I'm only sixty-one years old. I'm *fine*.

He wants to stop the pitching balcony, the woods advancing toward him. He's had premonitions before, at each of the touchstone moments of his life: the day his father was killed, that was the first one, and then the whole week before his mother died. The morning of Beatrice's accident and that awful March day when Hallie left him. Shaking himself, he adjusts the pillow in the Adirondack chair, pulled close to the screen the way he likes it, and sits.

Anxiety needles through him: Cordelia is flying in from South America, old friends whom he hasn't seen in years are coming, and Beatrice—he can't help worrying about her. Travel can be stressful, and he doesn't like her to put additional strain on her body. It's ridiculous really, all this hoopla, more than he's ever experienced for the opening of a building. "But it's the first retrospective the Weisman Museum has ever done on a Minnesota architect," Hallie reminds him. "You should be proud."

He *is* proud. His firm has won more than its share of competitions and awards; he believes he's living up to the aim he had as a young man to be a great architect, to elevate, in Louis Kahn's words, the circumstantial to the ideal. If he doesn't always achieve it, he continues to try. Not once has he ever considered lowering the bar. Maybe it's the word itself, *retrospective,* that bothers him—the focus on the work achieved, the career already made. Finished. Isn't that what's implied, a career past its prime, the best work done?

It pisses him off. As good as he is, he can and *will* do better. His partner, Alex Thorne, laughs at his frustration that the Weisman exhibition will only be shown at a handful of museums around the country. "Don't be so greedy," Alex says. "What do you expect, MoMA?"

"Good, yes," Hallie says. "Excellent, yes. But who goes through life wanting to be *great?* What does it even mean?"

He knows what it means to believe yourself capable of being among the best. He wishes Hallie would understand. She's happy for him, happy, too, that their daughters and her sister Clare are coming. It seems small and ungrateful to be pissed off when such an honor has been handed him. And now everyone's coming and there's so much yet to do: his speech, a new door for the shed, the garden.

He finds this looking back sentimental, a waste of precious time, though he's learned to keep this to himself around Hallie. In the old days she would have said there was something wrong with him, that his emotional life was stunted in some essential way. For her, past and present are indistinguishable. "That's because you're a poet," he says in his own defense. And yet the memories keep coming. The ones of his father leave him restless . . . wanting. Wanting what? An apology, maybe: *I'm sorry for the pain I caused, the mess I made of our lives.* He's startled by a gust of wind and leans forward in his chair, the sighing pines stirred out of their uncharacteristic stupor.

As suddenly as the unexpected breeze comes a flood of images. He shakes his head to ward them off but they press forward, whispering and insistent: gold on metal, blue water, pinwheel umbrellas on a crowded beach. His father, Tommy Fens, rolls down the window in his yellow Karmann Ghia and tilts his face into the salty air. Sometimes Carl stops there, takes the story in a different direction, toward the boardwalk and beach where he and his parents spent so many Sundays when he was a boy. Now, however, he stays with the speeding yellow car, watches his father's chestnut hair scatter into the glittering embers on the tip of Carmen Festuccia's cigarette. Neither one saw the semitruck wandering like a lazy eye in the westbound lane. No time to stop or even swerve when the truck veered wildly toward them, plummeting down onto the yellow hood, a cataclysm of crunching metal and glass. The fire was so fierce that witnesses were forced to watch helplessly until a fleet of emergency vehicles arrived.

Carl was in third-hour Latin at St. Joseph's High School when nausea riffled through him and he gripped the side of his desk. Something terrible had happened. When Sister Regina appeared at the door, Miss Hanke, his Latin teacher, frowned at the interruption and trudged over in her rubber-soled shoes. Carl watched her gray head descend toward the principal's black veil. Both women's eyes turned sorrowfully in his direction.

"Carl Fens," Miss Hanke called out gently, motioning him over.

He closed his eyes, willing back the nausea. At sixteen, he was already six feet tall, and he slouched a little as he walked. Sister Regina laid her papery hand on the gray sleeve of his jacket, and the beige tile walls in the corridor lurched. The policeman's blue uniform was visible through the glass window of Sister Regina's office.

The officer was tall and overweight, about his father's age, with a silver crew cut and shiny number 47 on his badge. "Your father's been in an accident, son. A car crash on the parkway near Coney Island. I'm afraid he's dead. Your mother didn't take the news too well and she . . . well, she asked if I'd come over and tell you. I'm very sorry. I know what a shock this must be. As soon as you're ready, I'll drive you home."

"Was there anyone with him?" Carl asked.

The officer grew even graver then. "Yes, there was someone, but we don't know who yet."

"There wasn't any identification," Carl said.

"Maybe you should wait . . ." Sister Regina started but Carl held up his hand.

"There was a fire," the officer said, "so any wallet or purse she might have had was . . . well, everything burned."

"Everything?"

"Everything inside the car, son."

The nausea rolled into his throat. "It was a woman then?"

"Yes, it appears so. Your mother said it wasn't a relative, though."

"You told my mother about the woman in the car?"

The policeman and Sister Regina glanced at each other. "Yes. She asked, just like you did."

"You better take me home."

As Carl peers into the dark, he hears the owl and leans closer to the screens. Gurgling stream, crickets, wind. Odd how still it was when he first woke and now . . . He shivers. *HOO-hoo-to-HOO-ooo, HOO-hoo-hoo-to-WHOO-ooo.* The barred owl, hunched in a black spruce on the western edge of Echo Pond, readying for the hunt. If I were an animal, I would be *him.* He glances over his shoulder to the bed, wondering if the bird's haunting cries have awakened Hallie. Her breathing is soft and steady.

You just don't want to be alone, he tells himself. And why would he, resurrecting such sad memories? Walking up the steps to the front door of their Brooklyn brownstone. Pausing outside the apartment and counting slowly to ten. Partly to calm himself, his erratic beating heart, and partly to prepare. He hadn't let himself think about what the accident would mean for him and his mother, whether she would be able to survive the shock, or whether she'd be better off. No more humiliation over Tommy's infidelities, no more sadness over their lost love.

"I'm so sorry, honey," she said, "having to find out that way."

He knelt beside her and wrapped his long arms around her. She laid her head on his, black on black, her skin carrying the smell of lemons. People arrived: the priest, the mother of one of her piano students, several men from his father's furniture showroom, his best friend, Frank Rossi, bringing toffee bars from home.

Later, alone in his room, he pulled the cardboard box from under his bed and started work on a new birdhouse. The rhythm of the work took over, as it always did, life receding behind the images in his head. He constructed the roof from bamboo sticks and white tracing paper. Beneath each tiny window he created a perch out of Red Dragon chopsticks. He cut metal half-moons from the olive oil cans he'd filched from Mrs. Katsiaficas's garbage and strung them along the edge of the roof.

After he'd retrieved the peanut butter ball covered with waxed paper from the refrigerator, he mounted the stairs to the roof. A sudden breeze caused a carol of tinkling chimes, and the moon shone on an array of birdhouses hung from three clothes trees. He attached this latest one, batting it lightly before he stepped back to view his creations. *You could have given her a chance to recover before you saw that woman again. You could have said good-bye, could have swerved, could have leaped out of the car.* Nausea flooded over him and he slumped onto the black surface of the roof, gazing west toward Prospect Park and the Brooklyn Botanic Garden.

Carl tiptoes across the wooden floor and slides into bed next to Hallie, letting her warmth lead him toward sleep.

The next morning he trims alders along the banks of the stream while Hallie gathers wild lupine. After bundling the last pile of branches, he scans the landscape: the meadow with its zigzag path that leads to the summer cabin—the one-story house they bought from the estate of Alice Badenhope in 1976 where they lived for almost thirty years—then the pine grove and tall, slender house where they live now. Carl can hear Hallie humming as she works her way in his direction, the sucking sound of her boots. Her straw hat appears alongside the girls' old playhouse, perched on blackened poles that rise in a V over the stream.

The summer he built it, the girls were seven. He worked out the design on tracing paper while Beatrice and Cordelia hung on his arm or over his shoulder. A rectangular house sitting a few feet above the water, with a skylight in the pitched roof that would let in sunlight and enable them to stargaze at night. They shrieked with glee when they saw the Plexiglas floor he'd put in so they could watch the russet stream and its teeming underworld beneath them.

"We'll get you a telescope so you can see the constellations," he said.

"Can we sleep in it?" Bea asked.

"What about the bugs?" Cory poked her finger through the large window openings.

"We'll put in screens, goofy. You think I'd let you sleep out there with all those bugs?"

"We can sleep in it??!!"

They slathered him with kisses, danced wildly round the room. Even now he can feel their wet lips against his face.

Hallie bends toward the bank and plucks a sheaf of blue flag iris for her flower basket. As she stands, she smiles at him, her eyes the same lilac blue as the iris. He returns her smile and heads toward the vegetable garden. The wind carries to him the smell of larch and a dizzying blast of new-mown grass.

In the sunny rectangular plot flanked by pines, he's planted a vegetable garden. By midsummer you can walk through the arbor and down the path into a riot of color—his favorite garden

room of all. It was modest in the beginning, just enough vegetables and herbs for his own family with extra for friends and a
few neighbors. Over time, however, the garden took over the entire meadow. He now pays two local teenagers to help with the
weeding and watering; what he doesn't give away he contracts
with a neighbor to sell at the farmers' market in Spooner.

A crimson splash in the cool cone of trees, an aisle of red tulips
and narcissus, and he is inside a glade pungent with bracken. He
adjusts his eyes to the gloom and lets his gaze drop. There amid
the crumbling leaves and needles are the first violets, the rose-
colored moccasin flower and showy orchis. Hallie's voice calls to
him from the past: *Catch me, Carl. Here, over here!* A shiver runs
through him as he recalls wrestling her to the ground, her long
hair wrapped around his palm. Pieces of bark clung to her bare
back, her buttocks bruised with violets. He turns away, his legs
gone suddenly weak.

He remembers their first meeting almost thirty-five years
ago. He was standing on a sidewalk in Amsterdam watching
her at a tulip stand across the street. He'd just come from viewing Vermeer's paintings at the Mauritshuis museum and was
caught by her glowing copper hair and face, beautifully propor-
tioned and suffused with light. He crossed the street, startling
her by standing so close. He muttered something foolish and she
laughed, light spilling onto him.

He didn't see her again until that evening at the hostel, when
he went outside to ask the group of young people sitting on the
steps to quiet down. The window was open—it was too hot to
close it—and he couldn't sleep because of the noise. She held out
a beer to him, and he sat next to her on the steps. Her name was
Hallie Bok. She was completing a Master of Studies in literature at St. Anne's College in Oxford and had been traveling for

five weeks. He told her his wallet had been stolen in Oslo, and a pretty Norwegian girl he'd met there lent him a hundred dollars so he could get to Amsterdam, where he was waiting for money to be sent to the American Express office. She liked the fact that he was studying architecture. He had a list, he said, of the great buildings and gardens in Europe. His goal was to visit as many of them as possible.

"What have you seen so far?" she asked.

Dozens, he said, and ticked them off: the Pantheon and Hadrian's Villa outside Rome; Corbusier's Villa Savoye in Paris, his monastery of La Tourette; le Nôtre's Vaux-le-Vicomte; Mies's Barcelona Pavilion.

"Mies who?"

"Mies van der Rohe."

She smiled playfully. "I was just teasing—I know who he is."

He grinned. "I assume everyone's as obsessed with architecture as I am."

"I do the same thing: reel off the names of writers as if they're common vegetables."

"It'd be easy to fool me—I don't know much about poetry."

He could feel her studying him. "Have you been to any gardens in Holland?" she asked.

"Yes." He opened his mouth to name them but caught himself.

When he asked if she'd take a motorcycle ride with him, her eyes leaped. He retrieved his bike from behind the hostel and met her by the front steps. She wrapped her arms around his waist as the motorcycle gathered speed. Near the airport he pulled into an open field where they lay side by side in the twilit grass. Departing planes bathed them in a shower of light. She slipped a book out of the waistband of her shorts and read aloud poems by William Butler Yeats.

After they returned to the hostel, she stood on tiptoe outside the women's dormitory to kiss him. He put his arms around her and pressed her body into his, dizzy at the feel and taste of her. She handed him a slip of paper with her address in Oxford and disappeared through the swinging door.

The sun, now that he's out of the woods, climbs higher. He adjusts the brim of his hat and listens for the faint echo of Hallie's humming voice. What if he hadn't followed her to Captiva ten years ago? They fell in love with each other again in that little bungalow on the beach—it was as true and real as anything he's ever experienced. And yet sometimes he looks at her and has the feeling that she's thinking of someone else. It's ridiculous—of whom would she be thinking? He and Hallie have always been faithful to each other. With all the mistakes they've made in their marriage, at least they've never been unfaithful.

He tests the dryness of the soil and adjusts the sprinkler system. With the drought in its third year, he wonders whether he should cut back the size of the vegetable garden. The prairie and wildflower garden, all native plants, are hardy enough to survive without watering. But the vegetables demand significantly more intervention: enriched soil added to the sandy mix, steady watering. There are bans on sprinklers in the Twin Cities.

He weeds a few of the flower beds, redoes several markers obliterated by winter, turns and aerates the soil in the vegetable garden. The heat bothers him, which is why he tries to finish his outdoor chores early in the day. Black dots mar his vision, and his knees quiver when he stands. Cordelia, dedicated arbiter of the ozone level, says that the time is coming when they will have to build an awning over the whole garden, not stand for more than five minutes in direct sunlight. "You're crazy," he's told her, but now he wonders. It's odd that when he pulls out his hand-kerchief to wipe his steaming face, there is no sweat.

After he finishes with this end of the vegetable garden, he moves to the flagstone path that runs along the eastern edge. Winter has heaved up and cracked one of the stones. He removes it, levels the ground, and resets the flagstone. As he places his foot on the metal edge of the shovel, a palsy grips his lower body. He pitches forward, aware of a movement on the periphery of his vision and a blue blur—the blue of Hallie's eyes, or the blue alpines speeding toward him.

HALLIE

Chapter 2

Caddis Wood and Minneapolis (Mid-June)

Hallie touches her cheek to Carl's and slips out of bed. He's sleeping, finally. She tiptoes across the wooden floor and lifts a cotton jacket from a hook hanging on the wall. The air is fragrant with oncoming rain. Carl's flannel shirt is draped over the back of the Adirondack chair, pulled close to the screens. He was up several times during the night, to the bathroom and then hunkered in the chair, a dark shape against black pines. This insomnia is a new problem, and his color is poor. Perhaps it's only the anticipation over the retrospective, she thinks. She steps noiselessly down the curving wooden stairs.

In the kitchen she takes a piece of paper and writes down the lines that came to her upon waking. She stuffs the paper and pencil into a pocket, prepares a pot of coffee, sits down to check her e-mail and list the tasks still to be done before tonight's opening at the Weisman. Her sister's plane arrives at two, Frank Rossi's shortly afterward—they need to leave Caddis Wood by eleven to make it home to Minneapolis in time for everyone to shower and dress.

The coffee done, she pours herself a cup and leaves the house, following the mowed path through tall prairie grass to the summer cabin. She stretches out her arm to brush the felty tips. Rain clouds above but clear in the distance. She lets herself in the side door of the wraparound porch and moves quietly past the French doors to her and Carl's old bedroom, where Beatrice and Jack are sleeping. Her heart aches at the thought of Cordelia asleep in the sunny room she and Beatrice shared as girls. Though it's been three years since the fire, it is still hard to accept the fact that Tim is gone, that he's not snuggled in the bed with Cordelia or fly-fishing in the stream with his father and Carl.

The house is still. Standing in the center of the porch, she surveys the meadow with pleasure. *The house is full. My girls are home. We are here, together.*

She sits in Alice's old rocking chair and cups the warm coffee in her hand. Carl still chafes that she prefers the summer cabin to the new house. After all this time she still thinks of it as Alice's cabin, although Alice Badenhope has been dead over thirty years. Carl spent years designing the tall, narrow house tucked into the stand of white pine. Four levels to reflect the strata of life in the woods: the lowest level, the girls' bedroom, earth-sheltered on three sides, with a sliding door that opens onto the mossy floor of the pine grove; above that the ground-level kitchen and living area; then his and Hallie's bedroom, level with the rustling pine branches; finally, the upper story, their two studies, skimming the tree canopy and overlooking the stream. The pièce de résistance at the top: a small rooftop observation area where he can stargaze through his telescope.

I *do* like the house! she told him. It's beautiful. I *do* appreciate the study. I use it most of the year. Once the summer cabin is opened for the season, however, she moves her writing desk onto the porch and works. Here, where she's spent so many hours, so many happy sad years of her life. Where her days as a young wife and mother are as vivid as her life now, a woman nearing sixty, healthy if slower, still married to the same man, a man whose gifts are the subject of a public celebration, a man she fell in love with in that magical, storybook way, not a doubt in her mind, nothing in her vision but him.

She takes out the slip of paper and studies the lines on the page:

Once I, too, was afraid of the dark:
the deep descent, the alien world,
the long strands of my fate
flying off the spindle
like a flock of frightened birds.

Closing her eyes, she listens to the stream, pictures Persephone in that dark place, hunched by the side of a silver river. She scribbles fast:

What did I know of these forgotten
souls, who hold out their hands
and tongues for reassurance, for water,
for news of home?

There, she thinks, and tucks the paper back into her pocket. Hearing a telltale splash, she hurries back to the porch in time to see a doe leap out of the tangle of branches at the bend in the stream. It pauses by the orange prairie lilies planted along the stream bank. The nose twitches. *Is she smelling rain or me?* Hallie wonders how many of the people who have been invited will actually attend the opening tonight. So many gathering to celebrate a life . . . no, not a life, a career—a distinguished, accomplished career.

She didn't know when she married him what the work meant. A young man haunted by his father's early death, only the world inside his head keeping him whole. Given her own mother's failures, she was determined to put her family first. What would her life have been like if her mother had not abandoned them, if Carl had been more ordinary, less driven by the work?

The chair creaks as she rocks. It saddens her to remember the woman she was when they married: so much in love, so quick to anger, so hurt by Carl's absences, by his total absorption in architecture. Her anger and disappointment in him banked and flared for years. "You're a fighter," her father said when she was little, letting the unspoken words "just like your mother" hang in the air between them. She didn't mean to be so judgmental, didn't intend her anger to wound Carl the way it did. She just wanted the marriage to be how she'd imagined—a deep, consuming love, the two of them equals under the weight of it.

Just then a groan of bedsprings as Jack or Beatrice turns in Hallie and Carl's old bed. Hallie closes her eyes and remembers other mornings . . . sitting here in the chair, two cups of coffee down and pages written. Then the squeak of the crib as Cory, always the first one awake, stood up. A thud as her feet hit the floor, the creak of the other crib followed by a rattle and bang as Cory rolled over the top and onto Bea.

Their personalities were distinct even as babies. Cory, the older twin, the path blazer, devoured the landscape with restless eyes and busy fingers, hungry to know how things worked, wanting to take apart and put back together. Bea, born almost thirty minutes later, pushed into the world only when she had to. Her eyes gazed serenely up at Hallie, her imagination so rich she could lie in her crib for long periods of time listening to classical music tapes or amusing herself with a sunbeam on the wall.

Oh, to go back, just for a day, Hallie thinks, yearning for the crash of Bea's water bottle against the wooden floor, the patter of running feet. She'd teeter on the brink between disappointment that her time alone was up and the sheer joy of hearing them galloping toward her. Swiftly she'd push her coffee and notebook under the chair, just in time to catch first one and then the other as they clambered into her lap. Hands and feet everywhere and their faces, gooey with saliva, rubbing against her.

"Pancakes!" Cordelia hollered.

"Pancakes! Pancakes!" Bea repeated.

Yes, she thinks, letter pancakes. That's what I'll make when everyone wakes. *Get up, get up!* She wants to call out. She longs to smell them, to feel their skin next to hers. Amazing to think she ever could have tired of them, resented their hold, their constant energy and questions.

At the side door she slips on Cordelia's running shoes and exits. Past the compost, the small herb garden on the western side of the toolshed, and down the tufted hill to the footbridge, where she kneels and studies the rippled bottom of the stream, blue forget-me-nots. A breeze whiffles the tops of trees and she hears a rumble of thunder. Other noises: quail, the trill of tree frogs, the bullfrog's stuttering moan.

As if the garden has a voice that only some of us can hear, Alice wrote in her notebooks. Hallie finds herself frequently in this position, head cocked, listening. When the first drops come, she concentrates on the sensation as each raindrop hits her body, pooling there and trickling slowly across the surface of her skin. Thunder again and wind.

"Mom!"

Hallie looks toward the porch and sees Cordelia's tall, willowy frame gazing out across the sea of grass. A minute later she appears at the side door and lopes down the meadow path to the stream. Her white nightgown gleams against her dark hair and skin, her long legs and arms tanned and muscular from hours of fieldwork in her job as a research fellow at the Missouri Botanical Garden Herbarium. Hallie studies the fine, chiseled bones in her daughter's face. She's lost weight over the past three years—grief or hard work or just not eating enough. It's most obvious in her face, tiny lines scoring the softer skin beneath her eyes. A reserve there, too, as if a clear veneer has been brushed over the original, obscuring the animated range of her former self. It pains Hallie to see it, knowing it's part of the protection her daughter needs to ward off memories of Tim's death.

"We're getting wet!" Cordelia calls out.

The rain falls faster now. They twirl slowly on the bridge, faces tipped heavenward. Such smells, Hallie thinks, grass and earth and fish and bark. They stand as the rain flattens the thin cotton nightgowns against their bodies.

"Race you!" Hallie calls and sprints up the path. They giggle as they spill inside. Raindrops hammer the tin roof, resounding drumlike through the house. "How can they *sleep?*" Cordelia whispers. Hallie tosses her a towel and they shake out their hair, blot water from their arms and necks.

"I'm going next door to make breakfast," Hallie says.

"I'll come over and help as soon as I'm dressed. Want me to wake the others?"

"Nah, let them sleep. They got in so late last night. I'll keep the food warm in the oven. Your father didn't sleep well and it's going to be a long day."

"Is he all right?"

"I think it's all the excitement of the exhibition. They're making such a big deal out of it. Why?"

"He looks tired, older, I don't know. He's always thrived on keeping so many balls in the air. Hard to think Dad might actually be slowing down."

Hallie runs the short distance to the house. When they were little, it was so easy to fix things. You hide bags of jelly beans or Sour Patch candies under their pillows, lure the bad news out of them, scratch their backs to soothe away the grouchies. Nothing like a forest fire—its furious, snapping face—a car spinning out of control on the ice.

She assembles the ingredients for pancakes and sets the table for breakfast. Moving swiftly and with purpose round the kitchen, she glimpses herself now and then in the mirror: tall and slender like Cordelia, her steel-gray hair cut short. It took a long time for her wavy auburn hair to turn, years after Carl's. Only that one white streak in front that appeared in Hallie's hair while Bea was in a coma. Arriving at the hospital a mother with a catastrophically injured child, leaving weeks later with that shock of white.

Hallie cracks eggs into the mixing bowl and mixes the pancake batter. When the pan is hot enough, she drops one big C and a big B onto the surface. Side by side, perfect. The rhythm of the task soothes her, and slowly she builds the pile of letters, one for everyone. Thinking, as she always does when she's making letter pancakes, of her father: waking to the smell, bounding to the kitchen and onto the chair placed strategically beside him. He'd hand her the ladle and guide her hand as she poured her letters onto the frying pan.

Hallie's heart aches at the memory of her father and the collision of events the night he died—the birth of the twins and the first visit from her mother in fifteen years. *Mama*, she thinks, with a slide of unrelenting sadness. Three years ago Clare reestablished contact with Maeve and last winter convinced Hallie to come for a visit that included all three of them. The long weekend in Clare's Seattle home had gone as well as could be expected—Clare the facilitator, Maeve characteristically reticent but offering openings for them to vent, Hallie thawing out enough to talk without lobbing too many grenades.

Hallie slips the pancakes onto a platter and places it in the oven. Through the window she imagines snow falling, the way it did the morning her mother left. She fills the frying pan with soapy water, spatula clanging against metal, and other sounds appear like ghosts in her mind: the loose hinge on the bread box, clattering silverware, the telltale squeak of the kitchen door.

That day, as Hallie stood at the window peering down into the backyard, a figure appeared on the snowy stoop beneath her. Her mother was wearing her brown wool overcoat and black galoshes, carrying the beige suitcase. In her other hand she held a black pocketbook, the one with the gold, horseshoe-shaped clasp. Maeve descended the thickened back steps and waded toward the gate. The snow was so deep it clung to the hem of her coat. Slowly she turned her head and glanced back toward the house. The light on the garage across the alley shone on her pale face and ruddy hair, so like Hallie's own. Her gaze swept the house and yard, as if she were taking a picture in her mind.

Hallie ran down the back staircase and threw open the kitchen door. Her mother's coat was visible through the gate, moving away from her down the alley. Hallie leaped over the steps and onto the back sidewalk. By this time the vise in her throat was making it hard to breathe. It was like this in her dreams, waking to a gorilla at the foot of the bed, his ferocious, flapping feet, and she unable to scream for her father. She pressed forward to the gate, oblivious to the cold swallowing her ankles.

When she reached the alley, her mother was a dim form between garages. Hallie opened her mouth to yell—*Stop! Come back! I don't want you to go!*—but only a wheeze emerged. She stood until her mother disappeared into the swirl of snowflakes at the end of the alley. Racing upstairs, she found her father seated on the side of the bed, fully dressed.

"Stop her!" Hallie cried, pulling at his shirt.

He put his long arms round her. "She wants to leave, Hallie. There is nothing I can do."

"When's she coming back?"

"She's not coming back."

"Go, Daddy, go now! *Please.*"

He shook his head sadly. "It won't make a difference. She's . . . not happy. She needs to be free."

"Free for what?"

He sighed. "Well, to do her work."

"She does her work all the time. It's all she does. It's *me* she doesn't like, *me* she wants to get away from!"

She pulled away from him and attacked her mother's dresser, scattering the things Maeve had left behind: her ivory-backed hand mirror, glass perfume bottles, a bowl of seashells. Jacob wrapped his arms around her again and swung her onto the bed, holding her until she quieted.

Hallie cools her eyes, smarting with tears, against the glass. Sunlight stipples the red pine boughs, still glistening with rain. Carl's arm encircles her waist and he kisses the top of her head. "Letter pancakes. Why doesn't that surprise me?"

She leans her head back against his chest, loving the long, lean hardness of his body. "You didn't sleep well."

He sighs. "Too much on my mind. As my body gets older and slower, my brain speeds up. I'll be fine after the opening."

"Are you excited?" She turns and massages the deepest worry lines in his forehead.

"Sure."

The porch door in the summer cabin slams and Hallie moves back to the window. Cordelia and Bea are walking, heads together, through the meadow. A stranger might miss the subtle residue of Bea's old injury, a slight slackening of her right side, most evident in her face when she is tired or anxious, as if the two sides have shifted ever so slightly out of alignment. An almost imperceptible drag in the right leg, not really a limp, but Hallie can see it, can tell immediately if Bea has slept well or is worried or has a cold coming on. Are all mothers like this? Their attention to a beloved child so deeply ingrained it becomes involuntary, like a cough or sneeze, something they can't help but must, especially when the child comes of age and they have to let her go. For if they don't, if they hold on or protect too hard, whom are they serving if not themselves? As strong and independent as Bea is, the long-term consequences of such a terrible injury are not clearly known. So far, Bea has surpassed doctors' predictions of what she's able to accomplish. Except having a baby, which she wants desperately but her doctors advise against. Hallie pushes back her instinct to pull Jack aside and make him promise not to let that happen.

Uncanny how they do and do not resemble each other, she thinks. Beatrice resembling a younger Hallie, her long auburn hair pulled up in a barrette, fair skin sprinkled with freckles, eyes a deep cornflower blue. Cordelia, the taller of the two, bobbed hair almost black, so like her grandmother Nan Fens, with Carl's and Nan's olive skin and lucent brown eyes.

Another slam and Jack catches up to them on the path. He is wearing jeans and one of Carl's ubiquitous flannel shirts.

Coming up between the girls, he circles each one with an arm. Hallie looks at him with affection, thankful for the providence, or fate, that brought him into Bea's life.

Carl opens the door and they tumble in. Hallie hands Cordelia a bowl of blueberries and bends to take the pancakes out of the oven. The room expands to hold them all—their happy voices, their delight as they bite into Hallie's perfect pancakes. The strain of the night before drops from Carl's face and he grows visibly younger as the meal progresses. Cordelia, too, lightens as they discuss plans for the evening: who's coming, what shoes to wear, whether it's too late to get a hair appointment. The only shadow that falls upon them comes when Hallie breaks the news that Lucas and Livy McGaughey will not be able to join them after all.

"Why not?" Cordelia asks, her face falling. Since Tim's death, and his parents' decision to live abroad, the two families—once inseparable—have seen each other only on holidays.

"They planned on returning last week but, well, Livy is painting again and Lucas is volunteering at a local clinic and they're very sorry, they wanted to be here, to see us all and especially you, sweetie, but they decided not to leave just yet."

"They sound happy," Bea says.

"Yes," Cory says. "That's good. It's just . . ."

They wait, all eyes on her.

"It feels like they've forgotten about me, that I don't matter to them now that Tim's gone." She shakes her head. "I'm being childish, I know. I just don't want to *lose* them." She glances at Hallie, who returns her look. She, too, feels the loss. Not having Livy, her best friend for almost thirty years, here in the woods, five minutes away. She misses her with an almost physical ache, matched in its raw hurt by her sympathy over her friend's grief.

She doesn't know how long Livy will suffer so keenly the loss of her only child. If a longer sojourn in India makes it easier for her and Lucas, then she is grateful. Grateful too that the place itself hasn't driven Cordelia away, that she still loves being in Caddis Wood.

"But you haven't lost them," Hallie says. "They just need more time."

"I have an idea," Jack says. "When we get back to Minneapolis, let's go into town to one of those day spas where they do facials and massages."

They stare at him. "All of us?" asks Hallie.

Bea laughs and pinches his cheek. "You are a special boy, Jacko."

"Do they do men there?" asks Carl.

"Of course they do men," Jack says.

"I'm going to call right now," Bea says, getting up.

"Count me out," Carl said.

"Not a guy thing, huh, Dad?" says Cordelia.

"I'm a guy," says Jack.

Carl grins. "I have a speech to polish. I'll do the dishes, though."

"Done," Hallie says. "We need to be on the road in an hour."

Hallie takes a seat in the front row of the Weisman Museum's small auditorium. With her are the girls and Jack; Clare, resplendent in crimson silk; Frank Rossi; Carl's partner, Alex Thorne, and the junior partners in the firm. Although the retrospective is focused on Carl, much of the work belongs to Alex as well. The room is packed with people: staff from the firm, architects and landscape architects and engineers who have collaborated with him and Alex, dignitaries, friends. As the tributes follow, one after another, Carl, seated beside her, is visibly moved.

She is, too, not at the tributes but at the images of the buildings themselves, the way the camera has captured the elements of each particular design. Although she's seen them all, either in person or in photographs, it feels as if she's looking at something altogether new: the myriad changes and gradations of light; the constant shifting of the viewpoint in space; compressed entryways leading the viewer into lofty atriums; the craftsmanlike use of materials. The text on the screen underscores the signature characteristics of a Carl Fens building: understated calm and simplicity, a luminous physicality, discipline, attention to proportion and detail, respect for the latent energy of the site.

Carl lets out a low exclamation when Sverre Bergström, feeble now and needing a cane, appears on the podium, having traveled all the way from Oslo. As photos of the town hall in Bergen fill the screen, Hallie feels the old, bittersweet blade between her ribs. The excitement of that first competition, the winning design that introduced Carl to Sverre and began their long collaboration. Began as well the loneliness she was to experience in her marriage, the hurtful sparring that bookended each departure and return.

She remembers standing in their apartment hallway in her nightgown, one infant crying in the bedroom, the other whimpering in her arms—her face gray with fatigue, breasts engorged with milk, trying to slow his retreat out the door. As he turned away from her, she lunged forward, clutching his suitcase.

"Don't leave me," she pleaded. "It's only been three weeks. Please . . . *please*, don't go."

As he looked down at her, emotions rolled over his face: alarm, sympathy, affection. Closing his eyes, he breathed in slowly once, twice, and when he met her eyes again, his own had grown a dull, hard finish. He drew himself up to his full height and firmly extricated the handle of his suitcase from her grasping fingers.

"I have to go, Hallie. Sverre has set up a charrette in Oslo for everyone on the team. You don't seem to understand what winning this competition means—it could affect our whole future. Clare said she'd come if you need her. All you have to do is call."

"You promised not to travel right away. I need *you*, not Clare."

He kissed the top of her head and left. Just like that. As the door closed, Beatrice turned her face into her mother's leaking breast and rooted for the nipple. Hallie moaned in pain as the baby's fierce little mouth took hold and her milk let down, coming in so fast that Beatrice choked and sputtered, milk squirting everywhere. Within seconds the baby was jerking with hiccups and needed burping. By the time Hallie had her feeding again, Cordelia was mewling fitfully from the cradle.

After she'd settled Beatrice and sat with Cordelia on the other breast, she was weeping. She tried to calm herself, having read that her mood could interrupt the flow of milk and make the babies fussy. Ten minutes later, Cordelia's head dropped back drunkenly on her arm. Hallie burped her and laid her in the other cradle, both babies blessedly asleep. She hastened to the bathroom and closed the door, sobbing so hard she had to grab her stitches with one hand as she sank to the floor. She crushed a towel to her face and cried into it, feeling the pull in her belly and pelvis. When she was spent, she stretched out on the floor, the cool tile against her cheek.

Now, Hallie watches Carl's projects tick by one by one, takes in the satisfied *oohs* and *ahs* from the crowd, soft remarks about projects that others in the room have worked on or seen. She plucks the front of her dress as the tremendous industry, and loneliness, of those years return. She learned to do for herself and the girls, became adept at parenting on her own, but it wasn't what she wanted. Midway through the short film, Beatrice, seated on the other side of her, takes Hallie's hand and squeezes lightly, sharing her mother's pride and their common loss at Carl's absence—wanting, always wanting, more of him.

At dinner the family is seated with Frank Rossi, who is almost completely bald now. No matter how long and far both men have come from St. Joseph's High School in Brooklyn, it takes only minutes for them to resume the mannerisms and language of their former selves. Frank knew since he was a boy, he tells Hallie and the girls, that Carl would be a success. He covered the roof of the apartment building with birdhouses, built miniature houses out of cardboard and balsa wood, carried those little black notebooks around with him everywhere, sketching and making notes. "He could have been a musician," Frank says. "He had his mother's ear and sensitivity for it, and God knows, he had the discipline. But architecture called him."

Embarrassed, Carl steers the conversation elsewhere, and he and Frank recount a story about a summer camp in the Adirondacks, how at fifteen they jogged in their jockstraps past the girls' campfire.

"Jeez, Dad, you gotta be kidding," Cordelia says wryly.

"That's nothing," Frank says. "One summer your dad set so many fires on the roof of the apartment building that his parents sent him to the farm to shovel manure. I went with him, of course. Turned out to be an incredible summer. We both got laid. Dottie Dawson and her friend—what was her name?"

"How should I know? *You* slept with her."

"Dottie Dawson, that was her name?" Cordelia asks.

"Miss Dairy Butter at the state fair," Carl says.

"Why'd you set the fires?" Bea asks.

"Seemed like a good way to piss off my father."

"Why'd you want to piss him off?" Bea asks.

"He was sleeping with a woman who worked for him. I always knew when he was doing it. I would have done just about anything to upset him."

There is a moment's silence, as always when Carl talks about Tommy Fens. He excuses himself to sit for a while with Sverre Bergström and his son.

"I wish his grandfather could have seen this," Frank says. "He was the one who taught Carl how to make things, *how to take care.* The two of us would sit in his wood shop watching as he transformed a block of wood, covering us with wood chips and sawdust. He and Carl loved every part of that farm."

Toward the end of the evening, Hallie finds an empty chair in a corner of the river gallery and sits, nudging her new shoes off her throbbing feet. It's the first time she's been able to steal a few minutes to herself since the evening began. Carl is standing at the far end of the gallery, surrounded by people as he has been all night. Still handsome, with a quiet strength and confidence mixed with natural charm that draw people to him. Paler than he was at dinner, he's taken off his tie and unbuttoned the top buttons of his white shirt. It's strange to see him flagging, a man able to work on a project forty hours straight without sleep.

Just then a man passes across her line of vision. She sits up straighter and stares hard at him. Not as tall as Carl, heavier, wearing a tuxedo, with graying sandy-colored hair. Although he's walking away from her, there is something shatteringly familiar in the tilt of his head, the way he stops suddenly and takes the arm of another man. When he smiles, she stands up. The man turns in her direction and she can see his face clearly. She shakes her head, as if that will dislodge the rush of feelings, when she realizes that he is, in fact, a stranger. *Not* Eugene, no one she knows at all.

A low outcry startles her. At the far side of the gallery, a huddle of black-suited men surround a crumpled figure on the floor. Seeing Jack running toward the mix, Cordelia behind him, Hallie leaps up and hurries across the room. Carl is lying on his back, face the color of ash, arms and legs splayed out. His eyes are closed but flutter open as Hallie drops on her knees beside him. Jack kneels across from her, Carl's wrist in his hand. He's all doctor now, his brow furrowed, as he takes Carl's pulse.

"Should I call an ambulance?" someone asks.

"No," Carl says, trying to get up. "I'm okay . . ."

"Hold on," Jack says, pushing him gently back.

Hallie lays her hand on Carl's forehead, which is cool and clammy. "Jack?" she says, turning to her son-in-law.

"Could I have some water?" Carl asks.

"I'll get it," Cordelia says and races off.

"Your pulse is a bit slow, but your color's coming back. Let's see if you can sit up. Slowly."

Jack and Hallie each take a shoulder and guide Carl to a sitting position. He shakes his head, as if clearing it, but the awful pallor is gone. Just then Cordelia arrives with a glass of water, Beatrice a few steps behind. Upon seeing her father, Bea hunches beside Jack, her face drawn with worry.

"Daddy?"

"He's all right, Bea," Jack says.

Hallie sees the slight tilt to Bea's face: the left upright and more sharply defined, the right slacker, as if she's just awakened from sleep. How easily stress reawakens the old injury. With one hand Jack massages her right shoulder, makes a circle on her back. With the other he takes the glass of water from Cordelia and hands it to Carl. Under his fingers, Bea's face realigns, the right side's tautness restored.

"Think you can stand?" Jack asks.

Carl nods. By the time he's on his feet, a bigger crowd has gathered, including several of the museum staff. After reassuring everyone again that he's all right, they make their way to the elevator. Jack walks on one side of Carl, Hallie on the other. At the car, Jack helps Carl into the passenger side as Hallie slides behind the wheel. Jack takes Carl's pulse again and nods, satisfied. "Drink plenty of water and get a good night's sleep," he says. "Make an appointment for a physical, just to be on the safe side." They wave good-bye as Hallie backs out of the parking spot.

She stops behind a short line of cars at the exit.

"How do you know Dale Schumacher?" Carl asks.

She looks at him, puzzled. "I don't. Who is he?"

"He's a structural engineer we've worked with on several projects. I saw you get up when he walked by—you acted like you knew him."

Something—what?—in his eyes as he waits for her to respond. Her heart skips. "I thought I did, but I was wrong." She rolls down the window to pay the attendant.

As they leave the parking ramp, she glances at him, but whatever it was has passed. He's checking messages on his iPhone. "You feeling better?" she asks.

"Yeah. It's the weirdest thing, like a curtain falls over me and I'm out. If this is old age, you can have it."

When they're finally home, Hallie makes tea and toast and brings them to the bedroom. The color has returned to Carl's face and he talks animatedly about the evening, trying to process the outpouring of praise from so many people. She knows how uncomfortable he is with intimate shows of admiration or affection.

It takes only minutes for him to fall asleep. She lies next to him, listening to the room's creaks and hums. Unable to sleep, she slips out of bed and downstairs to the living room, where she wraps herself in the afghan and settles into the rocking chair. She touches her chest, feeling a whisper of the old arrhythmia, and thinks again of the moment in the gallery when she thought she saw Eugene Kinsella. The same clutch in her stomach that day in Captiva when Clare and Nathan introduced them. She'd heard about him, the friend whose wife had died. He'd rented a condo in Sanibel so he and Nathan could play golf and the three of them could sail. They invited her to come with them—sailing and then out to dinner.

She pulls the afghan close, twining her fingers through the openings in the weave the way the girls did when they were little. Yearning again, after all these years. She conjures his face, the sandalwood cologne he wore. During that first year, when they were writing regularly, she imagined she could smell him each time she opened his envelope. Carl coughs upstairs and she leaps up. Why would he just keel over like that? As she climbs the stairs, she makes a mental note to call the doctor tomorrow and schedule an appointment for a physical.

Chapter 3
Caddis Wood (July)

The stream carries their voices to him. Since the opening at the Weisman, he has felt as if a mysterious weight has infiltrated his body. He shakes himself, a small act becoming routine, like a nervous twitch. Tipping the jug of sangria so the flavors mingle, he hears footsteps mingled with the slosh of fluid and stops still in the narrow roadway. His heart is loud. He squeezes the canister tightly, willing the heartbeat to slow. As he turns his head slowly toward the shrubbery, he senses the big brown eyes before he sees them. Neither one blinks. Fur the color of bark. A sudden shudder as the deer turns, crashes through twigs, explodes upstream. The purr of water resumes and with it a peal of laughter.

Sunlight coats the green grasses along the edge of the road, ox-eye daisies, feathery clusters of yarrow. He anticipates the break in the shrubbery, catches sight of two black inner tubes, a bobbing gray head, and pale flicker of feet. Hallie shrieks his name with a wild pinwheeling of her arms.

"Carl, go to the middle of the bridge. Watch us!"

He shakes the canister vigorously and smiles. The road makes a loop past Katie Moran's vegetable garden on one side of the Clam River and Katie and Rick's brown cabin on the other. The mustard-colored shades are secured, signaling the Morans' absence this weekend. The rope swing curls in a slow figure eight over russet water. Pausing in the center of the bridge, he hears the clucking water, hears, too, Cordelia's giggle as she hooks her bare toes under Bea's black inner tube and bumps her sister against the muddy bank. Bea's auburn hair blinds him as he strains forward against the rail, trying to see their faces, the small hands that dart and circle in his memory.

"Carl!"

He reels around. Hallie and Clare appear at the bend in the river, paddling backward in black inner tubes. Their backs are to him, and he wonders, in the glare of sunlight, if they are naked— Hallie's slender back beneath her cropped gray hair, Clare fleshier, more olive in complexion, her salt-and-pepper hair a curly tumble on her shoulders. He grips the railing, aware of his rubbery legs, when suddenly in a dramatic whoosh the women dive forward, their torsos upside down in the water, naked buttocks floating directly beneath him like two perfect moons. Stunned, he gets them mixed up, and the two buttocks wiggle as the women struggle to free themselves. Hallie slides out first. Her body kicks free and she swims, surfacing a few seconds later with a sultry shake of her head. One arm grabs Clare underwater, and when she, too, surfaces, the two women howl with happiness. His light-headedness past, he leans over the railing and brandishes the canister full of sangria.

"Drinks on the veranda, ladies."

He grins at the sight of their naked bodies clambering up the bank.

"Carl, bring us our towels. They're right behind you . . ."

"You gotta be kidding me, and pass this up? Not on your life."

They shriek again as he pulls three paper cups from his pocket and arranges them on the railing.

"Come on, Carl, Clare's naked."

"Like I haven't seen her naked? Get your asses over here before the ice melts."

They rise, sashay hand in hand across the bridge.

"You saw me naked once, and that was almost thirty years ago, Carl Fens."

The sun is in his eyes as he glances away, remembering the splendid sight of their young bodies running lightly into the water. Sheepishly he reaches for a towel and drapes it across Clare's body. She cuffs him lightly on the arm. "So where's this fabulous sangria I've been hearing about?"

Carl pours them each a glass and leads the way toward the Morans' front deck, where they sit side by side on the steps.

"Whatever happened to the old guy with the walking stick who owned this cabin?" Clare asks.

"Earl Badenhope. He was a great-nephew of Henry Badenhope—you know, the man who owned our cabin. One of the nicest people in Caddis Wood. He was hit by a car while he was walking his dog back in the Cities." Carl shakes his head. "Tragic."

"What's more tragic," Hallie says, "is how long some people live, when they've been of little use to anybody, whereas others, needed and loved, go in a matter of minutes."

He thinks of Tim McGaughey: his valiant race across the meadow to save the Holman brothers, the fire faster than all three of them. Lucas's face when he and Carl reached Lost Creek and found Tim lying in the shallow stream.

"Are you talking about Mama?" Clare asks.

"I don't know how you can see her the way you do and not be . . ."

"Not be what?"

Hallie sighs and shakes her head.

"She's alone in the world, Hal, and getting older. I'd like her to feel comfortable in my home in case . . ."

"In case what?" Hallie asks.

"In case she needs to live with me someday."

"Clare! You don't need to take care of her . . ."

"Why not? Why wouldn't I?"

"Because she doesn't deserve it."

"She's still our mother, Hal, no matter what she's done."

Hallie shrugs. "*You're* the one she's comfortable with."

"When you drop the sarcasm she's comfortable with you, too. She loves talking with you about poetry."

"You know as well as I do that writing poetry is the most useless thing a socially conscious individual can do with her life," Hallie says.

"Why do you do that? Mama loves poetry. You're the one she gave her books to, not me."

"Okay to *read*, Clare, not to make a career out of. Poetry's only useful when it helps to relieve the human struggle."

It never ends, he thinks, these wounds we carry with us. Not for Hallie, whose third book of poetry is due out in the fall, her career in full gear, their children grown. Yet she still carries the ghost of her mother, Maeve O'Neill, who walked out on her family for the more compelling demands of the larger world, abandoned them without a word or visit for over twenty years.

And me? he wonders. Sixty-one years old and still haunted by a yellow Karmann Ghia and a mother who never stopped grieving. You think when you marry that you've left all that behind, your childhood and your parents' dumb mistakes. *Not for me!* you cry. *I* won't cheat on my wife. *I* won't neglect my children. And you don't—that's the beauty of it. You don't cheat. You don't neglect. Not in any way you recognize, anyway. But the hurt piles up. And then one day she phones you from Captiva. *I don't know if I love you anymore,* she says. You gaze at the wall, the emptiness so big you feel as if you're falling from a twenty-story building.

Hallie waves toward the bridge. "Cordelia! We're over here."

Carl glances up, instantly lightened at the sight of his daughter. She is strikingly handsome, with his mother's dark coloring and Hallie's tall, slender frame. She holds up one of her handmade plant presses. "I've found a heart-leaved four-o'clock, a dwarf ginseng, and a dame's rocket."

"Have some sangria with us." Carl refills his glass for her.

Cordelia has his long-legged stride. "Wait until you see what I bought in Spooner." She unbuckles her day pack.

"I didn't know you'd driven into Spooner," Hallie says.

"*Mom,* I told you earlier I was going."

He picks up the edge in her voice, the one that says, *If you were* really *listening, you'd have heard me.*

"Did Beatrice go into Spooner with you?" he asks.

"Nope, she's composing a Fourth of July arrangement for us." Cordelia lays out an array of fireworks: sparklers, firecrackers, Roman candles. "And Jack is preparing his Fourth of July chili."

"These days they choose men who cook," Carl says.

"What about you, Cory, any interest in dating again?" Clare asks gently.

"Cory's too busy cataloging plants to be thinking about dating," Hallie says.

"*Mom.*"

"I'm sorry, honey. I didn't mean . . ."

"Just don't do that, okay?" Cory turns to Clare and her voice softens. "I know you mean well, Aunt Clare, but I have *no* interest in dating anyone."

"Tell us about Ecuador," Carl says. "How many plant species did you find?"

"Eight hundred and fifty-seven. We would have gotten more, but . . ."

"Isn't that enough?" Clare says with a smile.

Cory shakes her head. "Not when you know that only a third of this particular rain forest is left. The rate the chain saws are moving, there might not be any trees standing the next time I'm there. We were after a certain tree—I won't bore you with the name . . ."

"Oh please, I love your names," Hallie says.

"*Minquartia guianensis*," Cory says, her voice thawing. "The bark is used to fight intestinal parasites, bronchial disorders, and tuberculosis. We found it, of course, but look." She holds out her right palm, pocked with tiny scars. "I was halfway up the tree when I put my hand right into a wasp's nest. You've never seen anyone rappel down a tree so fast."

"Does it ever get to you?" Clare asks. "Life in the field, I mean."

"Are you kidding?" Carl pours Cordelia another glass. "The more primitive, the better."

"Actually," Cordelia says, looking around the group. "I've been thinking of making a change."

"What do you mean?" Carl asks.

Cordelia turns to him. "Remember that landfill project I worked on in St. Louis?"

He nods.

"We consulted with a company from Cambria, Wisconsin, that specializes in ecological planning and restoration."

"I know the firm," he says. "Alex used them on a riverfront park on the St. Croix River. Are you thinking of working for them?"

"I don't know. Maybe. I have to finish the research I'm doing at the herbarium but after that, well . . ."

"You mean, you might be moving to Wisconsin?" Hallie tries to conceal the excitement in her voice.

"I said I'm *thinking* about it."

Carl stands. "Right now, we'd better hustle back before Bea thinks we've abandoned her."

As they pass Joe and Marnie Pratt's house, they hear the first, shimmering notes from Beatrice's keyboard. The music intensifies as they cross the last bridge and enter their lane. Carl adjusts his hat, feeling the sun beating on his head. A few yards ahead of him, Clare and Hallie keep a perfect, side-by-side gait. There is a glint of red in Hallie's graying hair, or maybe it's the rose-colored panel fluttering behind her. Sensing a movement in the green grasses along the road, he jerks his head round, hoping to sight a deer for Clare. *Nothing.*

He shivers in the heat, dodges black dots that shower the mowed lawn behind the white cabin. As he shakes his head to clear his vision, he sees his mother's aging hands on the keys of the baby grand piano. She gave lessons up until the day she died, of a massive heart attack, climbing the stairs to her second-floor Brooklyn apartment. When Hallie calls out to Bea, the music stops. A moment later there is a tumble of red hair in the doorway. Bea pushes open the screen, smiling her radiant smile at the sight of them. A chill rains over him, cold and then hot. Heat pours down his legs, soaking his groin. Bea's face clouds over and she wavers on the threshold, her eyes dropping. He gazes down at himself, his hands splayed open at his sides. His wet trousers cling to his thighs. Beatrice reaches out to him, her hands tentative and gentle, warm against his skin.

"It's okay, Dad. You've . . ."

Wet myself. Bea's face floats into a sea of women's faces converging on him, their eyes wide with horror. He would have made a joke, *Look at me, I've spilled the sangria,* only the empty sangria canister is still closed tightly, lying on its side against his foot, and it is the tang of urine he smells, not wine. A blurred movement again on the periphery of things, and he sees a man standing by the toolshed, a familiar tilt to his right shoulder, that wing of chestnut hair. Carl reels with dizziness. Hallie's eyes reach across the gulf and catch him, supporting him momentarily with their blue gaze. Then her eyes lose their color, as do the trees, grass, sky. He falls to his knees, head wobbling like a puppet's, and to the ground.

"*Jack!*" Beatrice calls, panic loud in her voice.

Carl is still conscious, rallies even as his body hits the ground. He struggles to get up, but their hands hold him back. When his son-in-law appears beside him, he is all business.

"I'm all right," Carl protests, sorry for the fear on Beatrice's face.

Jack examines him briefly and helps him up. They walk him slowly into the cabin, where Hallie fetches him a glass of water and props a pillow under his feet. "It's the heat," he says. "I fainted, that's all."

"That's *not* all," Cordelia says, glancing at his sodden trousers.

He shifts position, looks nervously at Jack.

"How long have you been doing that?" Jack asks quietly.

The ice, clinking softly in the glass of water he holds in his hand, pitches over the edge. Jack reaches forward and grabs Carl's right wrist, shaking as if with ague.

"Who is that?" he asks, pointing toward the window, the man clearly visible by the toolshed.

They turn their heads in unison, stare blankly, return to him with raised eyebrows, confusion etched on their faces.

"There's nobody there, Dad," Cordelia says.

"You're a bit disoriented still." Bea glances at Jack for affirmation.

I'm losing my mind then, along with everything else. He smiles lamely but can't pull himself away from the man he sees so vividly through the screen, who turns suddenly to face him.

"So it is you," he says softly. He rubs his eyes, throbbing and dry.

"Who?" Hallie leans toward him, taking his hand.

Chapter 4

Caddis Wood (September)

Hallie turns her laptop away from the late-morning sun. She's been downloading articles from the medical library at the University of Minnesota and surfing Web sites, hoping to gain some insight into Carl's illness. She's frustrated with the doctors they've seen so far. Looking up from the screen, she rests her eyes on the late-summer glow of the meadow. The midday grasses are on fire: crimson bluestem, golden switchgrass, straw-colored sideoats grama. Blazing among the bronzed, stiff clusters of goldenrod and yarrow are hearty sunflowers and dog-toothdaisies, coneflowers still in color. She sighs happily and drinks from her water bottle, loving the persistence of summer, the way it hangs on in the fading, somnolent heat.

Framed on her desk is a drawing of the late-season meadow taken from Alice's notebook, mirroring the view in front of her. She showed Carl the drawing that first summer, soon after they'd bought the property from Alice Badenhope, when he was immersed in the renovation of the cabin and his grand scheme for a country garden.

"Why mow it?" she asked him. "Why not work with what's here?"

He glanced at the drawing and smiled indulgently at her.

"They must have burned the meadow regularly in the old days to keep back the weeds." He motioned to the overgrown alders crowding the banks of the stream. "I'm going to clear this out, reshape the edges of the stream. Wait until you see the flower beds I have in mind!"

He'd already gutted the inside of Alice's white cabin; framed in a new kitchen, bathroom, and laundry room; extended the porch around the western corner of the house; taken a buzz saw to the wall and cut in an opening for French doors so their bedroom opened directly onto the porch. Then he mowed the tall, tangled prairie grass and wildflowers, and seeded the lawn. Carted in topsoil and fertilizer for his flower beds. Constructed netted coverings and fences to protect his shrubs and flowers from hungry wildlife. Bought pesticides and herbicides to ward off marauding pests and weeds.

The garden became a local showpiece. Still, it often felt to her as if he were engaged in a full-scale war: he and his flowers and lawn against the insects, weeds, and predatory animals determined to eat or destroy what he had planted. Twenty years later, in that spring after she went to Captiva, he dug it all up—the lawn and hedgerows, his beloved flower beds—and planted a native prairie.

Hallie sighs with pleasure at the result and focuses again on the computer screen, scanning the abstract of another journal article. She is tired, but if she naps, it will be even harder to sleep and she's been sleeping so poorly already. Time enough this afternoon to finish packing. When Carl returns from work tomorrow, she wants to be settled in at home in Minneapolis. He doesn't like it that she's coming back early on his account, her habit for years now to stay on her own in Wisconsin through the end of September, him coming out on weekends, but even he cannot deny how impaired he is. The two-hour drive to Caddis Wood is out of the question. What if he passed out while he was driving? So far, when he's fallen, he's been able to get up, with only an occasional bruise as evidence. But what if he fell and really hurt himself—tumbled down the stairs, hit his head on the basement floor? Who would help him?

By the time he finally went in for a physical, she had made him a list of symptoms to give to Dr. Balfour, their regular physician. Flutter in the eyes, spasmodic motion in the hands, fainting spells, bladder incontinence, dry mouth, lack of sweat. She wanted to add his sightings of his father, Tommy Fens, which now included brief conversations, but he refused to let her. "He'll think I'm nuts," Carl said.

When he returned from his visit, he waved the prescription at her. "I've got a *bladder* infection. Doc says I'm getting older, I should slow down a little, take vitamin supplements."

"That's it?" she stared at him, incredulous.

"Everything else looks fine. Blood pressure's good, on the low side actually, heart sounds okay. He did some blood work, which will come back in a few days. You worry too much, Hal."

She groaned inwardly, frustrated at the doctor even as she empathized with Carl's obvious relief at the diagnosis. "What about the fainting spells?"

"It may be the low blood pressure. I have another appointment for next week, when all the tests come in."

In the weeks that followed, his symptoms multiplied. Dr. Balfour referred him to a colleague at the University of Minnesota. Carl saw one doctor there, then another. Finally, Hallie started her own research, with help from a friend on the faculty at the U of M nursing school, who was able to access the right journal indexes. "Keep a diary," her friend suggested. "Write down his symptoms, what happens day by day."

Hallie shuts off her computer and changes into hiking clothes.

With this gorgeous weather and no bugs, she's been hiking several miles a day. Over the past few weeks, she's covered all fourteen hundred acres of Caddis Wood, recording in her notebook the paths that need mowing, bridges to be repaired, downed trees to be removed. This is Marnie Pratt's responsibility, but Marnie broke an ankle a year ago, broke it again six months later, and now walks with a cane. Hallie was happy to take over the job. She is in the woods several times a week anyway, doing research for the association's long-range master plan.

After the fire three years ago, the members voted unanimously for a management strategy that would protect and preserve Caddis Wood. They hired consultants to assess the health of the trees and test the water quality of the river and streams. Each of the members has been given a forty-acre parcel to analyze: they are to examine the ecological communities and record their own histories with the landscape—personal anecdotes and memories, changes that have occurred over the course of the members' lifetimes.

When Hallie and Carl bought the property, her only way of coping with the strangeness of nature was to become its student. She wanted the forest to be as alive to her as it had been to Alice Badenhope, whose parents built the cabin soon after she was born. Each day Hallie walked the property with a camera and notebook. Gradually she learned the difference between bog and swamp, upland and lowland forest. She could identify individual trees and shrubs, native wildflowers and grasses, birds and butterflies. She tracked the forest through the seasons, took the girls with her when they were old enough, showed them how to dry and press wildflowers.

Her field notebooks are not only part of the members' collective attempt to protect the forest ecosystem, but also a link to the past—to her memories of life as a young wife and mother in Caddis Wood—to Livy McGaughey, whose paintings of birds and other wildlife brought Hallie back to her own poetry after the girls were born—to Cordelia and Tim, whose passion for nature, seeded as children, became an enduring connection between them and drew them to botany and forestry as professions.

She dons her straw hat and strolls up the lane toward the Pratts'. The sun is warm on her skin and she sighs with pleasure. The air is free of the flying phalanx of flies, mosquitoes, gnats, dust, and bees that plague her in summer. She walks past the Pratts', the old barn now turned machine shed, the meadow that in Alice's time served as pasture for horses. Marnie's laundry hangs in parallel rows of white on the grass behind the house. The road curves and rises into the deeper woods.

Involuntarily she turns off onto the McGaugheys' road and hears the tinkling of Livy's wind chimes. As she nears the house, she anticipates the moment when the meandering road widens into meadow, the broad horizon, the McGaugheys' old log cabin to the left, and on the right the elegant lines of the cedar and glass house Carl designed for them. Bird feeders hang empty from the eaves, and in the meadow, bluebird houses perch like lonely sentinels. She gazes across ruddy grasses to the winking creek at the bottom of the hill and then, to the east, the white pine grove where Tim and the girls built their many forts. Two years older than Bea and Cory, Tim had his mother's honeyed hair, his father's steadiness, and an irrepressible imagination. The twins acquiesced to almost anything he asked of them. In return, he led them to his many treasures: trees with branches low enough to climb, soil packed with foot-long night crawlers, a pileated woodpecker's nest filled with three perfect eggs in a rotting red pine trunk.

Don't worry, Hal, we can see the fort from the window.

Hallie looks up at the deck, thinking for a brief second that she actually sees Livy standing in the doorway, her thick hair pulled up in an unruly tumble, her welcoming smile.

"Oh, how I miss you," Hallie whispers and climbs the few steps to the deck. She recalls the August day when she met Olivia McGaughey for the first time on the trail leading to Echo Pond. Carl had told her about them, the couple who owned the cabin overlooking Sand Creek: the wife a wildlife biologist and a painter, the husband a doctor, a six-month-old son. Hallie recognized her right away, the tall, handsome woman carrying her baby in a backpack. *Stop in for coffee on the way back,* Livy sang out.

Hallie lifts the sundial on the corner of the deck and takes the key tucked underneath. Letting herself into the house, she smiles at the shifting planes of light that flood the interior. She glides across the gleaming wooden floor to the hand-painted table and runs her hand across the top rung of a ladder-back chair, remembering the afternoon she and Livy painted the chairs outside on the deck. Livy's easel leans against the wall across from her. On the wall behind the easel is a painting of a great gray owl on the verge of flight in the twilight woods.

"I was wondering if you'd write a poem for it," Livy said one day, sitting across from her at the kitchen table. "I've got a show coming up in October in Minneapolis. I want to submit some of my birds—there's a woman from Rodale Press I've been corresponding with, and she'll be coming to the opening. It's a mixed-media show and I'd like to have poetry to accompany the paintings. What do you think?"

"I've only just started writing again." Since the birth of the twins, Hallie had only written in her notebook, nothing that resembled a fully realized poem.

"So?"

"Even if I weren't so rusty, I don't know enough about birds."

"Sure you do. It's better to bring a fresh eye to it—you're more open to the bird, then."

After the twins were born, she was in a state of inertia with her writing. At the time she was grateful for relief from the ever-present pressure to publish—not just individual poems, but a book. Relentless submissions to the handful of literary and university presses that still published poetry, contests and awards sought after by every emerging and midcareer poet in America. Livy's invitation shook her out of her cocoon and gave her an excuse to turn away from the internal chaos of her own story—its layers of sorrow and loss, the constant torment over the love/hate/guilt she felt, feels, *always will feel* for her mother. As hard as she tried, she always ended up believing she was writing the same poem over and over again.

Then here, out of the blue, was this new subject matter and myriad rich, concrete nouns: *Yellow-headed blackbird. Hermit thrush. Mountain laurel.* Sounds, smells, sensations that, after the birth of the twins, permeated her newly susceptible body like a tuning fork. As if her heart and nerves had become carriers for all the wildness out there—all its whirring, chipping, humming, whining, whispering, rushing noise.

Day after day she filled her notebook with pure, impersonal images. Whatever nature offered up, she took. She moved away from free verse, created patterns whose formal constraints shifted the focus away from herself. She experimented with the *ghazal*, the sestina, the villanelle. As the forest wove its way into Hallie's poems, she became more and more preoccupied with the borders between nature and humans, nature and art. She wanted to slow time down—one word, one line, one couplet and stanza at a time.

"If you're not happy with the poems, the show will go on regardless. What have you got to lose?" Livy asked.

Hallie sighs, drinking in the presence of her friend. Those poems, which led to her first book, taught her how to enter her own life obliquely. They gave her a renewed understanding of music and tension in the line.

Hallie walks from room to room. She's avoided this—the happy hours she and Livy spent here taking care of their little threesome, mediating squabbles, sharing the ordeal of Bea's injury, surviving adolescence and the slow-dawning realization—*how could we have been so dumb?*—that Cordelia and Tim were falling in love. Overseeing their simmering relationship until that glorious Saturday wedding in Caddis Wood.

With a sigh, she closes the door behind her and leaves the house. She hikes through the woods to the logging road leading to Echo Pond. Livy's red ribbons still adorn the trees along the path. She turns down the Sour Bean Trail, part of the forty-acre piece she and Carl are responsible for. With pen and notebook in hand, she logs the diversity of trees, documents the ones that are stressed or have fallen. As she progresses along the trail, she notes the range of ferns and club mosses; tall and low shrubs; harebells, wild geraniums, and large-leaved asters. She doesn't hear as many birds as usual, not a single scarlet tanager or rose-breasted grosbeak. She hasn't heard a whip-poor-will since their first years at Caddis Wood.

After she's done, she hikes back up the trail and down the path along the ridge overlooking Echo Pond. She sits on the alder bench built by Henry Badenhope over fifty years ago and weaves her fingers through waving stalks of big and little bluestem. Tamaracks circle the pond in a belt of golden lances. A gust of wind releases the last leaves on the creekside alders and ripples the surface of the water. Everywhere she looks is afire: early gentians, brambles, lanternlike leaves on the blackberry bushes. In the distance she hears a woodcock's twitter and the *cooo, cooo, cooo* of a mourning dove. She closes her eyes and sees the shadow cast by her husband's tall profile as she raced down the hill over thirty years ago.

Carl was standing in a small rowboat in the belly of the pond, stark naked, casting toward the bank. Hearing her voice, he sat down and rowed toward her.

"You don't care if someone sees you out here?" she called out.

"Only you, baby. Hop in. No, wait." He put up a hand. "You have to be naked. It's the rule."

"Whose rule?"

"The rule of the boat. See?"

He lifted one leg to show her. There, written in charcoal pencil on the inside hull of the boat were the words *Naked passengers only.*

"There is something seriously wrong with you."

He grinned. "Time's wasting, Hal."

"I'll get eaten alive."

"There are hardly any bugs out in the middle. The wind keeps them away."

"What if someone comes?" She fingered a button on her blouse.

"There's nobody out but Lucas McGaughey, and he just headed over to the Clam. He won't be back this way. I *promise.*"

Quickly she stripped down. He laid a towel on the seat and helped her in. Languidly, he rowed them toward the heart of the pond. Once there, he put the oars up, spread the towel on the sun-baked bottom of the boat, and lay there, his back against one side of the hull, long legs hinged over the other. The sun was high in the sky, but with the breeze it wasn't too hot. The boat drifted gently, water sucking against the sides. He stroked her lower back with his hand, ran his fingers across her leg and down the inside of her thigh. "Come down here with me, Hal. I get lighthearted just looking at you."

"I don't have my diaphragm with me."

"One time won't matter . . ."

"You wish."

"So what if you get pregnant? We want kids, right?"

The lake was a multitude of colors: blue gray in the sunlight, ocher nearer the shore, burnished brown as she peered down over the side of the boat. Swallows airplaned over the polished surface. She caught the shadowy outline of her face in the water, and then his hand closing on her hair.

Hallie takes off her straw hat and brushes the back of her head, startled for a second at the feel of her bare neck instead of the long auburn hair. She didn't want a baby then, not with her father dying and Carl so busy starting a practice. What if she had worn her diaphragm that day and had a baby a few years later? Not that one blessed egg dividing into two. Not Cordelia. Not Beatrice. A stab of worry hits her and she stands, hiking up the slope toward home.

When she reaches the summer cabin, she Googles the Mayo Clinic and goes immediately to their Web site, where she studies the list of the doctors' specialities. What she needs is a private investigator—in medicine—someone who'd know what questions to ask and where to look.

A sudden rush of warmth floods through her, and she shakes her head, wondering why she didn't think of it before. When his wife got sick, Eugene took a leave from his job and devoted himself to her treatment. Clare and Nathan swore he kept his wife alive longer than anyone expected. It's what he *does,* she reminds herself: he's a microbiologist who researches diseases.

She enters her and Carl's old bedroom and sits down on the floor beside the antique bureau that belonged to Alice Badenhope. The bottom drawer is where she keeps Alice's notebooks, arranged in chronological order—from the first notebook Alice started in 1924 to the last one in 1974 not long before she died. Behind the notebooks is a shoebox that Hallie lifts out and sets on her lap. In it are two neat bundles, each tied in ribbon: the thinner one, the letters Eugene wrote during the first year after Captiva; the second, the cards he sent each year thereafter for her birthday and Christmas.

She has a sudden twinge of guilt as she holds the letters in her lap, thinking of Carl's curiosity the night of the retrospective, when he thought she knew Dale Schumacher. She shakes it off, refusing to feel remorse over something that seemed so inevitable at the time. She didn't tell Carl about Eugene, not when Carl came to Captiva, and not afterward. By then the romance with Eugene was over and she believed it would do more harm than good to tell him. The letters—well, they were innocent enough, two friends keeping in touch. After they built the second house in Caddis Wood, she moved the letters here, to the bureau in their old bedroom.

She wonders if other women would think her reckless or naive for not destroying them. You don't know my husband, she would say. Carl never went through her things, didn't pay attention to what came in the mail for her, who phoned, where she went during the day. She used to resent this trait in him, thought it indicated a lack of interest in her, lack of love even, but she learned over time that it was simply who he was. The everyday details of her life held no meaning for him. And since he was never home on a weekday, and rarely on Saturdays, she ran little risk of his ever intercepting the mail.

She could e-mail Eugene—the address would be easy enough to find at the University of Washington—but she decides to write in the old way. The letter is simple and to the point. She summarizes the trajectory of the disease, its odd symptoms, using her diary to make sure her description is accurate. She tells him briefly about each of the girls, says she is well, that her third book will be out in the fall. She asks after his wife and stepchildren. Slowly she writes out his address, the house he and his wife bought and renovated a year ago. *It has a view of the water and a narrow beach where I run with the dog in the mornings. I still think of you. Eugene.*

Later, after she's finished packing and eaten the last of the soup she made the night before, she walks back up the lane, turns right at the car bridge, and heads toward the summer gate. It is her favorite time of day, soft and quiet, gold-stippled, the forest easing toward dusk. If Carl were here, he'd be fly-fishing north of the car bridge.

Hallie opens the mailbox and slides the letter inside. Hearing a car, she steps back from the road, between the mailboxes and the red iron gate. Joe Pratt's pickup lumbers by, raising dust.

"Want a ride?" he calls out, slowing down.

She waves him on with a smile and turns into the woods, knowing the trails—deer path and human—by heart.

Chapter 5

Caddis Wood (December)

It is midafternoon and the snow is still falling—thick, papery flakes that paint the air with dots. The ground has been rising steadily; the new snow swallows the paths Carl shoveled only this morning. Slowly he peels an orange, arranges the cool, fragrant pieces in a meandering line along the window ledge. It is an old habit. Not that he does it on purpose to annoy Hallie. He simply loves the sensuality of fruit, its smell and taste and texture, the act of placing the peel in that particular place beside the glass. He should go out and shovel, for if he waits until it stops, the snow will be too heavy to lift.

He doesn't mind shoveling again. The activity bends his mind away from his fear, a sweating animal that pounces several times a day. As he zips up his jacket and closes the door behind him, he glances through pines to the summer cabin, the long front porch blinded by mustard shades, a light in the living room signaling Hallie's presence. She does this often, now—retreats to the cabin to read or write. She keeps the wood-burning stove going until late afternoon, when she returns to start dinner for the two of them.

He grabs the shovel and walks slowly through the grove in her direction. She is sitting at the desk facing the window, but her head is bowed over her laptop, and he recognizes in her rapt face, even before he sees the movement of her fingers on the keyboard, that she is deep in it. Since he's fallen ill, she's had a hard time concentrating on her poems. He's told her that it's up to the doctors, not her, to find out what's wrong with him. But that's like talking to a wall: once she's fixed on a project, there's no stopping her.

He remembers the terrible days after Beatrice's accident, Hallie sitting by the side of the hospital bed, not leaving, not sleeping, no matter how hard he or Clare or Livy tried to reason with her. Not even Cordelia, numb with grief and fear like the rest of them, could move her. Hallie believed that Bea was waiting, cocooned in her coma, for the right moment to emerge. In the interim, Hallie stayed by her side—reading to her, singing, rubbing her body with lotion. After Bea emerged from the coma, Hallie hung on like a bulldog to the belief that Bea's brain damage would be minimal, that, with the right amount of inspiration and enrichment, she'd catch up. Of course, Bea did more than that, or the accident did, stimulating parts of the brain so that her sensitivity and musical ability deepened exponentially.

The table behind Hallie is strewn with books and papers. He can just make out the faint strains of the Pachelbel Canon. A flutter of wings as a red cardinal lands on a slender birch twig, plucks a brown bud, and soars off, bud in mouth. Carl turns from the window and sees across the road the far edge of his grandfather's cornfield and through that a line of trees. He brushes the snow from his face and looks again. The white igloo beneath the pines is his fort. He and Frank Rossi built it the winter following his father's death. In the clearing west of the fort, they scattered pieces of bread and birdseed. Lying behind the wall, eyes glued to the small aperture Carl had carved out, they waited for the

chickadees, the juncos, the male and female cardinals. As the
wet flakes drop lightly onto his face, Carl feels that other wall of
snow against his forehead.

When Frank motioned to him, he shimmied over and peered
at the glossy photo of Miss February in Mr. Rossi's latest *Playboy*.
The cold pages crackled as the boys turned them. Once they finished, Carl crawled to the far edge of the fort and uncovered
their arsenal of homemade guns. Next to Frank's magazines,
their favorite pastime was setting up skirmishes in the woods.
Leaving Frank behind the wall, he grabbed one of the stripped
alder limbs and sped into the trees, heading for the ditch they'd
dug a week ago. Soon the woods resounded with shots. *Rat-a-
tat-tat. Rat-a-tat-tat. Kerpoom. Kerpoom.*

Steady tapping on the glass startles him, and he jerks his head,
seeing Hallie's querying face against the window. He shrugs his
shoulders and trudges alongside the house to the path leading
to the road. He begins to shovel, swiftly falling into a familiar
rhythm: large sweeps that funnel the snow from left to right.

It would have been nice living here during Alice Badenhope's
time, when Caddis Wood was a working farm and the meadow
in front of the Pratts' held grazing cattle. On winter weekends
he snuck into his grandfather's barn when everyone was asleep.
Cows munched lazily on the hay, big and warm in their yeasty-
smelling stalls. After murmuring a greeting to his favorites, he
padded along the wooden floor to the section of the barn where
the new calves were lodged. He loved their knobby heads and
depthless eyes, the way they took his two fingers into their open
mouths and sucked hungrily.

Carl stands upright on the path and wipes the wet snow from
his face. Only it isn't snow that sticks to his glove, but tears and
mucus. He glances around sheepishly, but there's no one in

sight. When he reaches the side door of the summer cabin, he sees Joe Pratt making his way from his pickup through ridges of packed snow.

"If you want, Carl, I can do this with the snowblower. I'd be glad to add you to the list."

"Thanks, Joe, but I'm still able. The exercise does me good."

Joe nods politely. "I'll be by tomorrow to fix the window in the shed."

"I didn't know it was broken." As he looks up, he sees the broken pane staring back at him. "Hallie ask you to fix it?"

"Sure. I ordered a new exhaust fan for the wood shop, too. Got your mail here. Marnie baked you some carrot bread." He hands over a pile of mail and a foil-wrapped loaf, still warm. "Darn, I forgot the CDs. A new bunch just came for you. I'll drive back and get them."

"Don't bother, Joe. I'll pick them up tomorrow. Thanks." Carl waves as Joe trudges back toward his pickup. He wonders how many other things he's missed or left undone. He flicks through the magazines and advertisements, pulls out a letter, postmarked Seattle, that is addressed to Hallie. He holds it at a distance to see better. Handwritten to Ms. Hallie Bok, the return address *Eugene Kinsella, 4231 Linwood Lane, Seattle, Washington.* Who's Eugene Kinsella? he wonders. As he leans his shovel against the side of the cabin, he has the sudden, shivery sensation that his father is behind him. *If I'm really dying, if that's why you've come, then you must have a role to play. Go ahead and play it, and we'll see what happens.* The odd thing is, he's gotten used to his father's spectral presence, has begun to count on his being there. It's not wise to count on his father, but he's sixty-one, so what harm can Tommy do him?

Whenever he enters the summer cabin, he feels a momentary disappointment that Hallie has chosen to work here rather than in the beautiful study he designed for the two of them on the top floor of the new house. "There's a letter here for you—someone named Eugene Kinsella."

She's halfway across the room, having risen from her desk and moved toward him when he entered the house. She freezes a few feet away from him, her face going still as glass.

"Hallie?"

She reaches her hand slowly forward and takes the letter from him, staring fixedly down at it.

"What's the matter? Who is he?" As he reaches forward to retrieve the letter from her, she turns her shoulder to him. He is confused. Hallie stands up straight and looks right at him. "It's nothing, honey. He's a friend of Clare and Nathan's and, it's silly—I had this weird moment—you know, thinking it might have something to do with Clare, that maybe something happened to her."

"But surely Clare would call you if . . ."

"Of course she would. Let's go next door and I'll make us dinner." She walks back to the desk and turns off her laptop.

"But why is he writing to you?" he asks.

"Oh, Clare probably gave him my book. I'll read it later."

He opens the door to leave but just as he hits the cold outdoors, he glances back over his shoulder and sees the light go on in their old bedroom. Curious, he slips back into the room and across the floor to the bedroom door. She's kneeling next to the bureau, putting the letter into the bottom drawer. He opens his mouth to ask what she's doing but stops. Something in the flat plane of her face, the furtive cast to her body, unnerves him. He strides back across the room and out the door. Midway across the yard he waits for her, takes her arm so they can walk the rest of the way together.

Back in the main house now, she busies herself in the kitchen while he lights the fire and puts on a CD. Sitting at his desk, he reads his latest e-mails. A feeling of unease has roiled through him and now, as he clicks through his mail, he tries to figure it out. Why would she put the letter in the bureau rather than bring it back here to read? They have no secrets from each other— oh, there are plenty of things they don't talk to each other about, but they're incidental, having to do with one or the other's work, things that don't really affect their life together. So why would she say the man is a friend of Clare and Nathan's, that it's probably about her book, and then hide the letter? Isn't that what she's doing, hiding it? Which is weird. Unless . . . unless *what?* He clicks on an e-mail from Alex Thorne.

Alex has forwarded a request for a proposal for a new river research center on the banks of the Mississippi River east of downtown St. Paul. Carl skims through the text. He's familiar with the site, the old Pig's Eye dump that sits on a wetland next to the river. It's all overgrown grass there now; he remembers a creek, trees—a pond or lake? Yes, Battle Creek flows through the site, discharging into Pig's Eye Lake. The proposal for a research center and surrounding landscape will need to address ways of cleaning up the site. He scans the data. It looks like everybody and his brother's been involved at one time or another in trying to figure out how to restore the place. The Minnesota Pollution Control Agency closed the dump in 1972.

Hallie places a steaming cup of tea by his arm and runs her hand through his hair. He looks up at her, the light catching the pale down on her cheek. His chest flutters and he thinks he should ask her rather than worry about it. Ridiculous waste of energy to blow things out of proportion. He shakes his head. He's never heard of the man—he lives in Seattle—Hallie goes to Seattle every few years—she hasn't taken a single trip he doesn't know about. *Just ask her.* What if she lies? But Hallie doesn't lie—it's not in her nature to lie.

See what happens when you let your imagination get the best of you? He watches as she chops and then sautés onions and garlic, moving swiftly between the stove and the spice cabinet. She doesn't look like a woman who's hiding something. He reads through the documents Alex has sent him. Almost twenty years of waste has been deposited in the Pig's Eye dump: household garbage, demolition waste, drums filled with PCBs and other hazardous substances, lead-acid batteries, heavy metals, sludge ash, industrial and home chemicals.

The dump is so big and so deep that it's impossible to remove or rebury it. Plus, it's located on a floodplain and underground watershed so that in a high-water event, there will be so much water that it will be very difficult, if not impossible, to pump it out or cover the waste with an impermeable barrier. The list of challenges goes on. Because the dump never had a permit, it cannot be cleaned up under the state's Closed Landfill Program. It is, however, a state Superfund site, which means there's at least two million dollars from the state for cleanup, but this will pay only a small percentage of the estimated cost. The Superfund is a "polluter pays" program, so the rest of the money should come from the parties responsible for the contaminants. At Pig's Eye, however, this is almost impossible to determine since thousands of individuals and businesses deposited contaminated materials on the site over so many years.

Carl whistles through his teeth. He can tell in every word and pause in the writing how much Alex wants this project. He grins, feeling the familiar rush of adrenaline coursing through his body at the challenge of a new and difficult project. At the end of the long e-mail, Alex writes: "The point of the center will be to focus on research and education about the Mississippi River, but the site itself isn't about the river alone. We'll have to figure out how to clean it up, and then how to build on it. Our proposal should integrate the site remediation as well as the design process."

He likes it that Alex hasn't said *if* we can clean it up. Of course not. Every problem has a solution; it's how they've always approached their projects. The bigger the problem, the more rewarding the design.

"Yes," Carl writes back, "so the center becomes a laboratory of sorts not just for the restoration of the river but for restoration of the landscape as well. Call your ecological planning contacts in Wisconsin. We may want to use them as part of the team."

"You haven't touched your tea," Hallie says. The room is fragrant with clove and cinnamon, the hearty smell of tomatoes.

"Are those our tomatoes?"

"Yep. I've still got a couple of jars under the house."

He nods happily. "What are you making?"

"Lentil soup and salad."

He sends his e-mail to Alex and then furtively, feeling like he's doing something wrong, he Googles "Eugene Kinsella." There are many Eugene Kinsellas, so he Googles "Eugene Kinsella, Seattle" and the screen fills with entries. Three photographs pop up and he clicks on one, glancing over his shoulder to make sure Hallie is still occupied in the kitchen. The first one is too small to make out much—a head shot of a man about their age, ashen blond hair. The second one pops open, a full vertical view. The man stands half facing the camera, his body partially turned to a gleaming sailboat behind him. There are evergreen trees, water, what looks like a marina or harbor behind him. He is smiling broadly. Handsome, Carl thinks, an outdoorsman, shorter than Carl but broader in the shoulders, muscular.

"How long till we eat?" he calls out.

"About ten minutes," she says.

He clicks on the first entry, the one from washington.edu, and reads. Another photo, this one more formal: tweed sport coat and dress shirt, same big smile. Eugene Kinsella, Ph.D. in microbiology, full professor, research in microbial biodiversity. He skims the rest—several pages of published articles, two textbooks, conference proceedings. Carl adds the word "wife" to the tagline and up pops an obituary: "Nadine Kinsella, Cellist at Seattle Symphony, Dies of Cancer." Married twenty-two years when she died, no children, active hiker, sailing enthusiast, member of the board of directors at a charter high school for the arts.

He gets up slowly and ambles over to the refrigerator. He can feel the warmth of Hallie's body a few feet from him. As usual, she is humming. "How about a glass of sherry?" He reaches for the bottle in the cabinet above his head.

"Um, yes. Would you put on Segovia?"

He pours them each a glass then walks to the shelf where they keep the CDs. As he takes the CD out of its case, he drinks in the smell of orange, sees the row of peels he'd left earlier along the window ledge. He remembers the feel of Hallie's arms around his waist as they sped along fuchsia-lined roads to Slea Head. Two days earlier they'd heard Segovia play during a concert in Dublin, then driven to Dingle, where they found the relative of Hallie's mother in a little whitewashed house facing the harbor. After, they headed to a house owned by the manager of the hotel in Dingle, who'd taken a liking to them and given them use of a cottage overlooking Great Blasket Island. From

Hallie's backpack he smelled the oranges they'd just bought in a tiny grocery in Ballyferriter.

Hallie shrieked with delight at the gray cottage surrounded by dry rock walls. Across the road, cliffs plunged into a leaden sea where in the distance hunched the three humps of Great Blasket Island: *An Blascaod Mór.* He rolls the syllables round in his mouth like pieces of ice. Later, Hallie peeled the oranges and fed them to him, one slice after another. Candlelight ignited her hair, made sparks in the black square window beyond which three dopey cows lumbered.

They'd never made love like that. The sound of waves through the open window, their sweating skin beneath the eiderdown quilt. Something turned in her that night, like an orange—rind and zest removed, delicate membranes visible inside the sweating pulp, and then you insert your thumbs into the tiny mouth and pull, exposing its moist, moon-shaped organs. As she kissed him, as she thrust him deeper inside her that night, he felt the caul dropping from his own heart, releasing a surge of freedom so exhilarating it made him cry out. Will he ever feel that way again? Every cell, every bone, every nerve ending awake?

After they've eaten, they settle next to each other on the couch and play four, five games of euchre. She's lit a candle that flickers in the black square window. As he studies her face, he can see every age in her—twenty-one, forty, fifty-eight. Once or twice the letter in the summer cabin darts into his consciousness, but he pushes it away, refusing to think of anything but the present, the two of them side by side in the room he's made for them.

In the dream he is kneeling at the window in the bedroom where he sleeps at his grandfather's farm, the room that used to be his mother's. It has her things in it: the quilt on the bed his grandmother made, the doll dressed in blue taffeta, the desk she used for school. The boy Carl looks out on the white fields, feels the wintry glass against his forehead, and breathes in the spicy fragrance of his grandfather's pipe tobacco filtering up from downstairs. His grandfather is reading aloud the Psalms: *Yea, I would wander afar, / I would lodge in the wilderness, / I would haste to find me a shelter / from the raging wind and tempest.* Suddenly in the field he sees his mother. She is wearing a flowered dress and she's walking away from him, toward the barn and the far grove of cottonwood trees. He calls for her to stop, to turn around so he can see her. She doesn't hear him, doesn't turn around.

When he wakes, the room is dark and he is hot, but as usual when he becomes overheated now, there is no sweat. He reaches for the glass of water on the nightstand and drinks. Turning toward Hallie, he is startled to find the bed empty. "Hal?" he calls out. When she doesn't answer, he calls again, louder this time. He gets up, puts on his robe, and descends the stairs. His eyes are accustomed to the dark now, and the moon glows faintly on the surfaces of things. Standing in the middle of the living room, he calls to her again. Alarmed, he walks to the window, toward the blink of light winking through the pines. It is their habit, when one stays up longer or is awakened in the night and can't go back to sleep, to descend to the living room or kitchen, turn up the fire, and read. Sometimes Hallie writes. Her laptop, he remembers, is in the summer cabin. He turns to go back to bed, but something stops him and he shivers. Putting on his coat and boots, he leaves the house, closing the door softly behind him.

If it weren't for the curiosity mixed with alarm pulsing through him, he would drink in the beauty of the moonlight on the snow, the black sky studded with stars. Light beams from the bedroom.

He treads lightly to the window and peers in carefully, not wanting to be seen.

She is sitting on the floor directly across from the window, her back against the wall, the bottom drawer of the bureau open. She has a letter on her lap but she isn't reading. She is lost in thought, her gaze fixed on some object in the room or on the rug. The glass is grainy with winter grime so he can't see her face plainly. Her body is slumped to one side. The letter moves involuntarily in her hand and she runs her right palm over it. His heart flutters, skips a beat.

He paces back and forth alongside the house. He should go inside and confront her. *I woke up, you weren't there, I saw the light in the cabin, I got worried.* He looks in the window again. She is up on her knees, bending over the bottom drawer. He hikes quickly across the snow and back into the house. Carefully he puts his boots away, wipes up the moisture from the snow he tracked in, is back in bed when she comes in. As she slides back into bed, he pretends to be asleep.

When he does sleep, finally, he dreams that he is inside a concrete block house in the middle of the woods. There are no doors and the windows are locked and made of such heavy glass he can't punch his way out. There is no furniture in the room, nothing to use to shatter the glass.

As he looks outside, Hallie glides out from the trees and begins walking in a circle around the house. She is far enough away that he can't make out the features of her face but he knows by her hair and body that she is young. She is wearing a summer dress, like the one his mother was wearing in the earlier dream. He bangs at the window, calls out her name, but she doesn't hear him, doesn't look in his direction. When she's made one circuit of the house, she turns back toward the woods. A man is standing there. Carl can't determine the face or age of the man, but as Hallie reaches him they turn and walk together into the trees.

The next morning she is up and dressed, making breakfast when he awakes. He is stiff when he gets out of bed, and his joints ache as if he's coming down with something. It feels like cotton is stuffed in his head and there is an uncomfortable tightness in his chest. For the first time in ages, he cuts himself shaving and swears, dabbing a tuft of Kleenex on the tiny wound. Each time he remembers the night before, his stomach plummets. He's never felt like this before, never had a reason to be jealous or to mistrust Hallie. Even when she left him that winter and went to Captiva, it was about the failures in their marriage, about *him*, not about another man.

She seems normal enough at breakfast, a little pale. They make small talk. She's already gone on the Web to read the paper and fills him in on the headlines.

"What are your plans this morning?" he asks.

She scrunches her face, thinking. "I thought I'd write a bit—had a good run yesterday. Though I have a book review to finish—I just wish I liked the book better. It's a first book of poems and I hate to give it a bad review."

"No walking today?"

"Why, you feel like a walk?" she asks hopefully.

"No, I have to phone Alex this morning. Maybe later, though." He smiles at her, acknowledging her fondness for their walks together. "I just thought, if you were going Pratts' way, there's a box of CDs there for me."

"I'll get them." She stands, starts clearing the table.

"You don't have to. I can ask Joe to drop them off later." He helps her load the dishwasher.

"I don't mind." She leans toward the window and gazes across the snow. "It's nice out. I'll take back Marnie's pan, thank her for the carrot bread."

A half hour later, he watches her walk across the path and around the summer cabin to the road. Quickly he throws on his coat and boots and walks rapidly over to the summer cabin. He can just make out her yellow scarf through the trees. He takes off his boots, walks lightly across the wooden floor in his wool socks.

Kneeling by the bureau, he pulls the knobs on the bottom drawer. It sticks and he recognizes it as the bureau that used to be in the living room—where Hallie keeps the extra blankets, linens, odds and ends. Once he tried to find a sweater in there and she laughed and pointed to the trunk in the corner of their bedroom. The photo albums are in the second drawer—he remembers that. He has to coax the drawer to get it to slide all the way out. Except for a pile of white linen napkins, the drawer is full of notebooks, Alice's notebooks, stacked neatly on their sides.

There's nothing lying on top of the notebooks. He squeezes his hand down between the notebooks and the face of the drawer and feels, but there is nothing there either. Pulling the drawer out farther, he sees a shoebox sitting behind the row of notebooks. Gently he lifts it out. It's an old shoebox, closed with a thick rubber band. He takes off the band and opens the box. Two stacks, each tied with string. One is all postcards and cards, the other letters. On the top, not tucked in either pile, is the letter from yesterday.

He sits down, knees drawn up and his back against the side of the bed, and opens the letter. It is short, handwritten.

Dear Hallie:

I'm sorry it's taken me so long to respond to your letter. I didn't have a chance to read it until a few days ago. Laura is on sabbatical so I took time off as well and we hit the high seas. Finally got the chance to do some extended sailing. We spent the holidays visiting my stepson in Madrid—he's there for a semester.

I am very sorry to hear about Carl's health. You were wise to send me so much information. It sounds like something is wrong with the autonomic nervous system. Some of the symptoms are similar to Parkinson's. The lack of sweat is an interesting detail. I've called a friend of mine who's at the National Institutes of Health in Bethesda, Maryland. He has some ideas but would need to see Carl to make a diagnosis. He'll make time to see him as soon as possible (Dr. Steven Schlain, 301-402-9612, ext. 429).

Thanks for letting me know about the girls. Every time I go to the orchestra I wonder if I'll pass Beatrice and her husband unaware. She's the one who most resembles you, Clare says, so I look, hoping to see her, if only to see a likeness to you.

Please let me know what you find out with Carl, and if I can be of any help.

Eugene

He reads over the letter again, slowly. A light has been lit beneath his heart and he feels it ricochet out of rhythm. Hears his own ragged breath. *Who is this man? When did they know each other?*

He lifts the two packets and shuffles through them, studying the postmarks. The letters start in April 1996 and end in September of the same year. The cards are regular for a while—twice a year—her birthday and Christmas—then just Christmas.

He flexes and unflexes his hands, fighting the urge to read them. He's never searched through Hallie's things, never read her mail or opened her e-mail. Such an invasion of privacy is repugnant to him. Yet here, in his lap, he feels like he's holding a stick of dynamite. To leave it alone is as horrifying to him as lighting it.

If this man, Eugene Kinsella, started writing to her in April 1996, that would have been right after they returned from Captiva. She'd already been there for several months when he followed her, determined to win her back, having taken the first leave from his business in twenty-five years. She didn't mention having met someone. He assumed she'd been with Clare or alone. He stayed in Captiva for five weeks. Other than those weeks in England and Ireland, after they'd met, or later, just after they were married, they'd never been so close to each other.

He turns the packet of letters over in his hands, as if by feeling the paper against his skin, he'll be able to intuit what's inside. Walking to the window, where he can see down the lane toward Pratts', he opens the first one. Reads quickly, ice forming in his chest.

Of course I will honor your decision. I am alone and vulnerable and you are still legally married. If things change, you know where to find me. I think of you every day.

The words blur in the watery light. *Legally married. If things change.* The man was *waiting* for her, believing there was hope for him, that their—Carl and Hallie's—marriage was bound by law only, not by love. A rush of nausea sweeps over him at the thought that she'd been intimate with this man during those weeks before he arrived in Captiva.

Just as he opens the second letter, he sees her yellow scarf through the trees. He hurries back to the bedroom, stumbling in his haste. He returns the letters to the shoebox, lays the letter from yesterday on top, and places it back in the drawer. There's no time to think of how he should handle this. Every nerve, every cell in his brain, is in turmoil.

He opens the door just as she reaches the side of the summer cabin and calls to her.

"What are you doing over here?" She turns toward him and draws nearer to the house. "Are you all right? Honey, you look awful."

"Come inside, Hal. I have to talk to you."

He holds the door open for her and steps back. As she passes she looks up at him, her face gone suddenly grave. She reaches her hand up to feel his forehead but he steps back, and her hand falls.

"Carl, what is it?"

"Take off your coat and let's sit down."

He chooses the armchair and she, impatient with her buttons, throws her coat across the back of the couch and sits on the edge of the cushion, facing him. He fights to keep his voice level. "I did something I shouldn't have: I found the letters in the bureau in the other room."

Her eyes widen in alarm.

"I saw you last night when you came over here and read the letter that came yesterday in the mail."

"You saw me—how?"

"I woke up and you were gone and I followed you. I was worried."

She shakes her head, trying to fit the pieces together.

"I needed to know who this man was, Eugene Kinsella, who wrote you the letter."

She stares at him. "How many letters did you read?"

"Just two—the one that came yesterday and the first one."

Silence hangs between them.

"Who is this man to you, Hallie?"

Her eyes dart away from him. "I met him that winter when I went to Captiva. Clare and Nathan introduced me to him. He's a friend of theirs from Seattle—he went to graduate school with Nathan. He'd just lost his wife and they wanted to take him to dinner with us to cheer him up. We became friends."

He knows who her friends are, certainly the ones who matter. "Why didn't you tell me about him?"

"It didn't seem important."

The tightness in his chest increases and he breathes in and out to relieve it.

"Why would he refer to you as 'still *legally* married'?"

"Our marriage was in trouble—you know that."

"You told him?"

"He saw that I was unhappy—he asked me about it. It was what drew us together—his grief over his wife, my unhappiness with you."

"Why would you tell a man you'd just met about your problems with me?"

"I told you—we were friends."

"Did you tell Clare about us?"

"I always talk to Clare."

"I mean *then*, that winter, after you said you didn't know if you loved me anymore."

She hesitates. "I don't remember what or when I told Clare . . ."

"But you remember telling *him*."

"You're making it sound devious—it wasn't. And it was so long ago. It was over before you arrived. I never saw him again. It means *nothing* now."

"*What* was over?" Her face doubles and swims. He blinks to clear his vision.

"Nothing happened, honey. It never went beyond . . . friendship. When I realized he had feelings for me, I stopped seeing him. I loved you—I told him that. I said you and I needed to work things out."

"And that if you couldn't, you'd go to him."

"I never said that."

"But he believed it."

"I don't think he really did. It was just something he wrote."

"You wrote to him. He wouldn't have written all those letters if you told him not to. You're *still* writing to him."

A glimmer of guilt shows on her face. "All we do is keep in touch now, once or twice a year."

"It's been ten years, Hal. That's a long time to keep in touch with someone who's not important to you."

Another silence. "We shared something at a pivotal time in each of our lives. I care about his well-being, that's all. He's remarried, he's very happy. I mean nothing to him."

"Is that why he says 'I still think of you'?"

She doesn't say anything.

"He was in love with you."

She tilts her head. "He thought he was. He was very lonely. He'd loved his wife so much and missed her terribly. It was the timing more than anything. If he'd met me when she was alive, he'd never have called me again. Even if we'd met a few months later, he wouldn't have been so open to it."

"And you? Were you in love with him?"

In the fraction of a second in which she hesitates, his world tilts. "No, I wasn't."

"Did you sleep with him?"

Another explosive fraction of a second. "No."

He shakes his head. He can't believe this is happening. "Get the letters then." He gestures toward the bedroom. "Read them aloud to me."

Her face, already pale, goes white. His chest is exploding.

"Carl." She breathes slowly in and out and her voice trembles. "What would be the point to that? He was a *friend*, that's all. I could never love anyone as much as I love you."

When she reaches her hand out to him, he pulls back, his body stiff. He gets up and walks to the closet, puts on his coat and boots. She stands in the middle of the room, her face stricken. "Where are you going?"

"For a walk. I need to think."

"Can I come?"

"No. I'd rather be alone."

"But what if . . ."

What if he falls in the snow? He's a child now to her, needing protection. And she, the good mother, will look after him as best she can. "I'm going alone."

There's a moment when he's walking slowly up the lane that he wishes she had come with him. His chest is as tight as a drum and his breath is all over the place and he wonders if he's having a heart attack. He concentrates on each step, focuses on the windblown brown reeds, the etchings on the surface of the snow. He thinks back on their weeks together in Captiva, how happy they were, how *real* it felt to him. Could he have been mistaken? Could she have fallen in love with this other man, *slept* with him, and then fallen in love again with *him*—as she says she did—all in the space of a few weeks? How is that possible?

He breathes in the cold air, trying to ease the weight in his chest. While he was agonizing over the fact that she might not love him anymore, trying to understand how things had gone so terribly wrong and what he could do to win her back, she was seeing another man. Sharing her feelings with him, putting their marriage—putting *him*—out of her mind.

As he turns off the lane and onto the path toward Echo Pond, he imagines her with the man in the photograph, the man with sandy hair and the big, enveloping smile. She'd be pulled in by that smile, that and her sympathy for him. A man who knew how to love, who would tell her things that he, Carl, wasn't good at. He thinks about the two of them in Clare's little cottage— did she make love with this man in the same bed *they* had made love in? Did she take Eugene to the end of the island and lie with him on the beach the way he and Hallie did?

His knees buckle and he drops, keels over in the snow. He's out only a few seconds. When he wakes, he rolls onto his back and gazes up through gray branches at the sky. A shadow blocks the sun, and his father's face stares down at him.

"Did you appear to her at the end? Kneel down with her in the dark? Is that your job now, to show up when one of us gets sick? Or starts to die? Is that it—I'm dying? Is that why you're here?"

The ground rocks beneath him and he flattens his hands against the snow to keep from sliding. He's inside a black cone, like the interior of a gigantic megaphone, spinning wildly. The ground is white and cold and there is no air, only a window at the top of the cone, a tiny square window to let light in. He forces himself to focus on the sound of the stream only yards away, its winking skin clad in silver scales.

As the ground stabilizes, he breathes slowly in and out. If his father did go to her, at least his mother wasn't alone. Didn't die all by herself in the empty stairway, unable to move or call out for help.

"I won't go gently," he says. "I'm not like my mother. I won't give up easily. I didn't cheat, either. Didn't break Hallie's heart by sleeping with other women." His voice breaks and he slaps the ground hard.

Was it duty that brought her back to him, or love? It if was duty, then their life together for the last ten years has been a lie. His face contorts. He has no tears so what passes for weeping is a dry, guttural heaving, as if he's being wrung inside and out. His father turns slightly, as if to give him privacy, and surveys the landscape, a tall sentry in the snowy wood.

HALLIE

Chapter 6

Caddis Wood (January)

Hallie wakes with one cheek glued to the open page of Alice's notebook. Others notebooks are strewn across the bed. She rouses and looks down at the page.

May 6, 1924

Mama and I worked in the swamp garden again today. "Nature's made this beautiful place, Alice, and we're going to help it along a little." We dug up several clumps of maidenhair fern downstream and planted them amongst the other ferns. Papa said there are plenty of ferns there already but Mama said maidenhair's the jewel in the crown. The path from the latrine down the hill to the stream is almost done. Papa and Henry laid the last fieldstone yesterday. "Little gold coins," Mama says, pointing to the marsh marigolds. They are her favorite spring flower but I love the trillium best. When I see their white hearts amidst the brown leaves on the forest floor, I know winter is over. If you pick them, trillium won't grow back. "Look but don't touch," Mama says.

She loves the way Alice's voice changes over the years. There is a lightness that never wavers, which Hallie believes is Alice's faith in the goodness of life. How did she keep this faith in the face of the sorrow she suffered: her son, Will, killed in Korea at the age of twenty-two, Henry dying in his fifties, the long years living alone in the house in Caddis Wood?

June 2, 1925

   We're building the wall tomorrow. Mr. Johanssen brought the rocks on Saturday in his pickup. Arthur will stay in Frederic with Mama to tend the store. As if I mind. This way I have Papa to myself and I can do what he tells me without Arthur butting in. He and Henry Badenhope, always bragging. Nobody can fish or play hockey like they do.

   Papa says the wall will be our memory place. He has things that he and Mama brought from Sweden. I don't know what to put in, but Papa says I shouldn't worry. Maybe I'll put in my best drawing of the whip-poor-will. Mama says we should come in at night when we hear the whip-poor-will call. Every night Arthur, Henry, and I try to find him but he hides too well and we never see him. Yesterday I heard him singing at dawn and crept outside and there he was perched on the woodpile. Arthur and Henry keep looking but so far I'm the only one who's seen him.

Hallie wants some of her own ashes put in the wall when she dies—Carl's, too. If he dies first, he said, she can put some of his ashes in the wall as long as she sprinkles most of him over Echo Pond.

Get on with it, she tells herself. She opens the bottom drawer of the bureau and replaces the notebooks. It is the first time she's been here since Carl discovered the letters, the first time she's left him alone in Minneapolis. He's falling regularly now; he walks in a lopsided way or he limps; the back of his neck aches so much at times he can hardly hold his head up. She bought him a neck brace but he won't wear it. He's sick of needles, sick of tests, of pills that make him feel worse. No one can figure out what's wrong with him. He won't admit, not to her at least, his fear that there's no end to his steady, relentless decline.

He has returned to the habits of their earlier life together, burying himself in work. A jury has selected five proposals for the new river research center in St. Paul—his and Alex's is one of them—for further design refinements. The winning proposal will be chosen in February. He's immersed in it, spending his days and evenings in the office. Given the pain he's in, she doesn't know how he's doing it. He sleeps in Beatrice's room now, won't look at her directly when he talks to her.

When he tells her he no longer trusts her, her heart palpitates with fear. Fear that he is seriously ill, that she may lose him, that he won't be able to get past it. His questions about her time with Eugene have brought it all back: not only her feelings for Eugene but also her feelings at the time for Carl and the loneliness and hurt she felt then in her marriage.

With a deep sigh, Hallie lifts the shoebox containing Eugene's letters and carries it into the living room. She stokes the fire and slides in another log. It crackles and fizzes, coating her with warmth. She places the lid of the shoebox on the floor and sets the pile of birthday and Christmas cards on her lap. She reads each brief handwritten note, then drops it into the stove, watching the paper brown, catch fire, and blacken into ash.

When all of the cards are gone, she lays the pile of letters on her lap and unties the blue ribbon. Her sewing box always had a ready supply of ribbons, long after the girls were gone from home. Ribbons saved from the years when one twin or the other was bound to want one to adorn a braid or ponytail. As Hallie reads each letter, starting at the last one and moving backward in time, the words resurrect the sound of his voice. Slowly he builds in her imagination until she can feel his breath on her shoulder, is able to inhale the sandalwood cologne he wore. Unlike Carl, Eugene was a man comfortable with words, with articulating his feelings. His *presence* was what struck her most powerfully in the beginning. He was completely there, eyes locked on hers, listening and at ease, no evidence that his mind was elsewhere. She wasn't used to it, this complete attention to the actual moment. It awoke in her an answering presence, pulled her out of the interior, hurt place she'd retreated to in her marriage.

Although Eugene was devoted to his work and his research, he joked about being a dilettante in another life. He loved music, which drew him to his wife and, in addition to their experience in graduate school together, to Nathan and Clare. They shared season tickets to the orchestra. He was an avid cook, he loved to sail, he was a voracious reader. He was very fit, a runner, although smaller and stockier than Carl. His thick hair shone in the sunlight. There was blond still in his beard, in the graying hair on his arms and chest. He was sensual: he loved the taste of food, ran his fingers over the contour of shells, licked the salt off his arm to taste it. He knew she was married, didn't ask if there was trouble in the marriage. He liked talking to her. Intentional or not, Carl's preoccupation with his work and neglect of her and of their marriage had eroded her confidence. There must be something wrong with her, she thought, she must not have enough to offer—was not smart or pretty or sexy enough—if her husband chose the work over her again and again.

She's reached the earliest letters now. The voice is different here—more vulnerable, plaintive even. They'd said good-bye to each other before he wrote these letters, three weeks before Carl

arrived. Eugene had behaved perfectly—of course he under-
stood, she was right to put an end to it, to work things out with
her husband. He respected her for that. Still, a part of him was
waiting; she felt it in the words he chose, his tone, all that was
left unsaid. He'd lost so much already in his life. It was one of
the things that drew her to him, the depth of his loss matching
his ability to love. Perhaps he simply could not bear to lose her,
too. Perhaps he could not believe that she could love her husband and experience such intimacy with him at the same time.

As she gazes into the fire, watches his words evaporating into
smoke, a wave of dizziness washes over her. She is sick with
memory—the cold, hard plane of glaciers and staggering vertigo, bands of shimmering seashells, poetry driven by the world's
suffering, questions that lodged beneath her eyelids like grains
of sand: *How can he love me if he's never here? Don't I deserve more
from a marriage than this?*

She was deep into a long poem sequence the spring she stayed
in Clare's guest cottage in Captiva. An immigrant girl, a ship, an
unrequited love affair, an abandoned baby. Other abandonments
as well: diseased children, children of rape, many forms of wildlife, the earth itself. Atrocities from the war in Bosnia were still
being uncovered. Without conscious thought, stories of mass
rape and murder entered the poem. Each time Hallie sat down
at her desk, she felt off balance, something awry in her inner ear.

The usual two weeks with Clare had stretched to four, then
eight, then twelve weeks. Monosyllabic conversations over the
phone with Carl, his voice distant and flat, like the chilly pocket
of her heart. As she gazed out the window of the cottage, the
room spun and lurched. Her dizziness matched the seasickness
in the poem, the disjunction in her characters.

How can you love someone that much, be such a deep and

important part of his life, bear and raise children together, and not love him anymore? *Does he still love me?* She didn't know, couldn't feel it from him. His hurt at her anger, her never-ending disappointment, had turned him inward and silent as a snail. He spent more and more time away or at the office. When he *was* with her, he was tired or preoccupied, his best self already spent. It hurt less not to need him, not to care whether he was there or not.

One day turned into another, until she phoned and told him she wasn't coming home. She couldn't say when. "I don't know if I love you anymore," she said. She looked down at the phone and felt like she was falling through space, down and down, no bottom to it.

By this time Clare knew there was something wrong, more than the usual conflicts. Hallie admitted there were problems, but *that's not why I'm staying.* It was the poem sequence she was working on, she explained, the girls were away at college and didn't need her, Carl was traveling anyway. She spun in place, hating this lie to her sister.

They followed their familiar patterns: eating breakfast on the deck, separating—Clare to the house to work on her latest article or her correspondence with clients, Hallie to the guest cottage to read and write—coming together later to walk on the beach, visit the cemetery behind the dunes, make dinner after watching the sunset. And then that fateful day when they met Eugene Kinsella at the edge of the water. Who better to cheer Eugene up, Clare said, than Hallie, who could be so warm and charming? Hallie saw it as a welcome diversion. She felt sorry for him, this man in grief over the death of his wife.

He drove more and more often to Captiva. When Clare returned to Seattle, she was surprised that Hallie was staying on, worried that something was happening between her and Eugene. Again Hallie obfuscated. "We're just friends. Neither one of us is looking for a relationship. You don't need to worry."

Every day he came. They walked for miles along the beach. He took her sailing. She hungered for the sight of him, the way his eyes brushed her skin, held her with total, steady attention. She could feel his desire for her. When she told him, finally, about her marriage, he didn't flinch. He was careful; he didn't want to be the cause of a worsening rift.

And then one day she kissed him, on the wooden walkway outside the cottage. He kissed her back, pressing her body against his.

Hallie grips the last two letters in her hands. Memory and regret course through her—desire, still, after all these years. The yearning to talk to him, to see him again. Not wanting, then or now, to let him go. She rocks in the chair and moans softly. It didn't matter that it happened fast or lasted for only a few weeks. Eugene's longing pulls at her from the page. Carl would be blind not to see it.

She reaches toward the fire then shrinks back, pressing the crushed ball of paper to her breast. She is stunned by her feelings, shakes her head to lessen the sting. After she said goodbye to Eugene, after she knew clearly and without doubt that she loved Carl, would always love him, she held on to their connection, to the memory of what happened in Captiva and the fantasy, alive in the letters, of what could have happened, might happen still.

You can love two men, she realized, the one you've loved since you were barely a girl, loved deeply and passionately and borne children with, and the one you meet in middle age, a man who makes you feel beautiful and young and talks to you in a way your husband never has. She is well aware of the power of her imagination, its ability to conjure up vivid scenes each time her marriage feels stale or predictable, when Carl works too much or fails to pay attention. *But aren't I allowed my fantasies, my unconscious life?* When she's deepest in, when the boundaries between inner and outer worlds disappear, she is at her best as a writer—completely awake and responsive. It is also, ironically, the hardest state to be in as a wife and mother, teacher, citizen of the world. You feel everything, and everything is magnified: every slight, every disappointment, every failure, every act of violence in the world. Over time she has learned how to live in both places at once, though one side or the other is almost always compromised. *We all have secrets, don't we?*

She tosses the last, crumpled letters into the flames, cups her head in her hands, and sobs. When she's done, she scans the darkening room, the black-limbed trees outside, flickering tongues of fire. Tossing in the shoebox itself, and then the cover, she pokes fiercely, willing the paper to burn brighter and faster, to leave no trace of itself.

It is past six o'clock when she walks slowly to Alice's writing desk, takes a sheet of ivory stationery, and writes. Her voice on the page is firm and clear. *Thank you for the name of your friend in Bethesda. . . . This will be the last time I write. Please do not write back, ever. I wish you only happiness, good health, a long and satisfying future. Hallie.* She seals and stamps the letter.

It is dark outside now, but she does not wait. The air is crisp and cold, fragrant with burning wood. It never ceases to amaze her how still and quiet the woods are, the ground thick with snow, dark trunks of trees, branches coated with white. The sky is clear with a bright half moon and stars, so she leaves the flashlight in her pocket. Her boots crunch on the hard-packed snow in the lane. Through the trees the lights sparkle from the Pratts' kitchen windows.

Just beyond the red metal gate, she pulls open the mailbox, hand-painted two years ago by Livy, and slides the letter in. She secures the latch and turns back toward home. She focuses on the physical details in the present: snow, trees, stars, her own breath entering and leaving her body, creak of tree branches, wind. Replays in her head what she will say to him. *Sorry. Wrong. Forgive me.*

CARL

Chapter 7

Minneapolis (February)

Carl searches through the drawers of his desk and turns to the files piled on the floor of his study. His rudimentary filing system has collapsed under the mountain of information he's amassed over the past few months. Trying to keep up with the myriad innovations in sustainable architecture is as daunting as it is exciting, and that's with a crew of architects and engineers participating. His mind reels with data: glass coatings, nanotechnology, rainwater collection systems, composting toilets, photovoltaic panels, wastewater reclamation, geothermal heat pumps—and that's only the *building* half of the equation.

Since the announcement three weeks ago that Fens and Thorne had won the river research center competition, he has spent his days in a fever. He's buried in it, driven like he was in the old days, pushing out of his mind everything but the details of the project. The illness, whatever it is attacking his body, is pitted against his and Alex's ambition to restore this almost impossibly contaminated landscape and design a sustainable building that will represent the best the firm is capable of. So far, his drive has put the illness in stasis, or at least it seems that way. He hoards his newfound energy, makes use of every drop, every minute in which his body is functioning near its old, optimal level.

Cordelia's decision to leave her position in St. Louis and take a job with Wisconsin Ecological Services has been another boon to his spirits. She's been assigned to the river research center project—the first opportunity they've had to work so closely together. It makes him happy to think about it. He hasn't been to the little house she bought in Brodhead, Wisconsin, but Hallie has, said that it's a cozy bungalow nestled on a tree-lined street and Cordelia has thrown herself into redecorating. A good sign, he thinks, remembering the bleak apartment in St. Louis she lived in after Tim died.

"What are you looking for?" Hallie has walked quietly into the room.

"The *wabi-sabi* book. It's here somewhere—I was just reading it."

She leafs through the sheaf of tissue paper sketches. "Here." Smiling, she hands it to him. "Can I see?" She gazes down at the topmost sketch. Black ink on white paper, the ink blurred where he's wet his finger and rubbed. "Remember that night in Cornwall? I came into the room after taking my bath and you were sitting on the floor with your sketchbook. You'd drawn a picture of the beach and done this." She points to the blurred ink. "I asked you why you did it and you said . . ."

"That when I wet the ink and rub, the ideas on the page take on the quality of living forms." He looks at her, remembering. Three weeks after meeting her in Amsterdam, he rolled his motorcycle onto a ferry sailing from Hook of Holland to Harwich, England. He found St. Anne's College in Oxford easily but had to wait for almost two hours until she showed up at the rooming house. She didn't seem surprised to see him and agreed at once to ride with him to the southwest coast. They watched the sun go down on St. Ives Bay and made love afterward in the little guest house on Bunker Hill Road.

They haven't made love since he found the letters. He doesn't know if his lack of desire is a result of the illness or the lingering mistrust he still feels. Plus, he's so weakened now he's afraid he'll be unable to perform. His anger dissipated after she returned from Wisconsin and apologized to him, honestly and without dissembling or excuses. Her feelings for Eugene were real, she said, but it was a momentary passion, filling in the leftover needs in their own relationship. The belief that it could actually lead to something lasted only a moment. "My life was always with you," she said. "I knew that even before you came to Captiva." Sorrow and regret emanated from her body like a fever. He wants to believe in her love for him, believe that what happened between them in Captiva was true and real. Hard as he tries, though, he can't recapture the faith he once had in their marriage.

"What are these?" She points to the topographic map of the site on which a grid of long, slender pins rises from the ground.

"Ground probes. Some are structural, others are biodegradable and will deteriorate over time into the water and soil."

"Will you explain it to me?"

"The contamination is compounded by the fact that so much of the site sits on a wetland along the Mississippi and is below the water table, so there's frequent flooding. It may not be possible to remove the metals in the soil and water—there are over a hundred times the legal limits of mercury and lead alone. The main task is to figure out how to remediate the site."

He points to the topographical map. "Which is where these ground probes come in. They'll be able to test the levels of contaminants in the water and soil. They'll also support a network of floating pods and walkways that will be suspended above-ground."

"Where will you put the research center?"

He points to a spot on the northern edge of the site, close to the river. She reaches for a sketch that shows a transparent cube floating on a number of thin columns in the trees. "Is this it?"

"It's just a preliminary idea."

"Are these probes as well?"

He nods. "They'll monitor the soil while acting as structural supports for the building."

"What's it made of?"

"Glass, recycled wood, steel. The building would be translucent—the floors and ceilings made of specially manufactured glass—so light can filter through as if through a canopy of leaves." He's excited now, the idea of it pressing at him. "These glazed cutouts would give a perception of depth and allow more light into the interior. Inside, people would be able to see or sense light in all directions—the horizontal and vertical planes in the building would disappear."

"Nice."

"Cordelia is bringing the latest analysis and recommendations from Wisconsin Ecological Services. She's coming this weekend—did she tell you?"

"Shall we all go out to the cabin?" Her voice is hopeful.

"Sure." He picks up his pencil and overlays another sheet of tissue paper onto the sketch.

"Are you coming to bed soon?"

He knows she wants him with her, both of them nervous about the conference call tomorrow. "In a while. I want to do more work on this."

She turns and walks quickly up the stairs. They're sleeping in the same bed again, a relief to them both. He fears he's wasting precious time by not making love with her, *time* the elephant in the room they don't talk about. Ten days ago she flew with him to the National Institutes of Health in Bethesda. "It's something in the autonomic nervous system," the doctors said, although they ruled out Lou Gehrig's disease. He should be grateful for that, he supposes. When Dr. Schlain's office called earlier in the day to schedule a conference call for tomorrow morning, he pressed the nurse to give him some idea of the diagnosis. "So, is it terminal?" He kept his voice light—*see, I can take it*—but she didn't yield, and set the call for 10:00 a.m.

He rubs his throbbing neck, sketches in a series of elevated walkways that lead to and from the building. Underneath the foremost tree in the site, he draws a bench and marks what he and Alex are calling a "healing ground." Cordelia and the other botanists and biochemists in her firm will create a garden there, using different plants to extract metals from the soil. The hope is that the plants will absorb the metals and other toxins through their leaves and roots.

He pulls out one of numerous sketches he's done of the space beneath the building. "Don't get carried away with the *structure as tree* metaphor," Alex tells him. He shakes his head. The two complement each other perfectly: Alex the more intuitive designer, Carl the theoretical one. Over the years they have debated, sometimes heatedly, the virtues of each approach, integrating them so seamlessly that it's no longer clear where one begins and the other ends. Carl wonders where Hallie put the neck brace, probably in the bedroom or bathroom upstairs. He isn't trying to fool anybody: the building is an artificial construct, *not* a tree, not a part of nature. He's not trying to change the unalterable fact that a building affects the earth around it. But why not design a building that does no harm, that is a light but powerful presence in the landscape?

He picks up his laptop and the book on *wabi-sabi* and carries them to the high-backed Eames chair. After adjusting a pillow behind his neck, he opens his teahouse file, a nightly ritual now that soothes him. He loves the juxtaposition of nature's soft shapes against the teahouse's geometric form. How time and weather increase rather than diminish the beauty of the structure. The small, unobtrusive building melds with its surroundings, doesn't try to make a statement that it's stronger or more durable than humans or nature. In one photograph, taken at dusk, the teahouse wall mirrors the silver and bronze striations in the saplings and shrubs nearby.

None of the spaces he visited in Europe gave him anything close to the out-of-body experience he had during the tea ceremony in the Byōdō-in temple in Japan. He was conscious of his mind receding even as he became deeply, painfully alert. Try as he might, he's not been able to re-create that feeling of simplicity and beauty in a building he's designed.

Carl shrinks the image and opens another file, one he created last summer when, on a whim, he returned to his grandfather's farm in upstate New York. The young couple who'd purchased the property had sold off the livestock and much of the acreage. They kept the back meadow and the old barn he and his grandfather had restored. It took the two of them two summers to complete. Together they probed and tapped the logs, looking for rot and other evidence of decay and insect infestation. They repaired or replaced the logs, seasoned the new wood, and rechinked the exterior by hand using a mix his grandfather had created to match the original. They took apart the old wood-shingled roof, which had suffered the worst deterioration, and put on a standing seam metal one. Carl finished the interior ceiling himself, using re-claimed oak boards and the original pole rafters.

His eyesight blurs and he becomes aware of his breathing and the beating of his heart. Glancing down, he watches his chest rise and fall. He winces with pain as he raises his head level again. Rather than ignore it, as he often tries to do, he concentrates on the sensations in his shoulders and neck, feels the tight, ropy muscle, the fiery ache. He closes his eyes and travels inward, try-ing to isolate each feeling inside his body. If he could probe the interior tissue with a small knife blade, tap along his bones, what would he find? Leaks or cracks or missing pieces, pockets of rot, small bulbous growths? A feeling of unease floods through him as he senses an infinitesimal movement deep within his cells, a hairline crack spreading ever so slowly.

He shuts down the computer. His neck is pounding. He takes three ibuprofen and walks into the living room, where he stretches out on the couch, bolstering his neck with a pillow. He'll wait for the pain to ebb before going upstairs to bed. When he closes his eyes, he is grateful that he no longer sees the image of Eugene's face or the lines in the letter that played over and over in his head for weeks: *I am alone and vulnerable and you are still legally mar-ried. I think of you every day.* Now, he pushes the images away if they reappear or if he starts to imagine Hallie and Eugene together. He thought about it relentlessly at first, needing to realign his own sense of reality with what was happening for Hallie that winter and spring. Knowing she was unhappy, even that she doubted whether or not she still loved him, was one thing—that she was able to put him aside and fall in love with another man was another.

Not that there hadn't been signs, that she hadn't told him how disappointed she was in him: his endless work, his silence, his failure to be there for her. He got so used to hearing it he simply stopped listening. She never talked about what he offered, what he *did* for her and the girls, only what he didn't do. In the beginning he told himself, *It doesn't mean anything, it's just Hallie.* Her need, her intensity, her anger. But the complaints, and her despair, intensified. He was off the charts, abnormal, unlike anyone she knew. *You're right,* he hammered back. *I'm not interested in what normal people do. It's not what I aspire to.*

It was her decision to stay home with the girls and only work part-time. He was proud that he made a good enough living so she had a choice whether or not to work. She didn't see it that way, said he made it harder for her, that if he was more available she wouldn't have to be so present for the girls, would have space in herself to write. What space did she need? He'd designed her a beautiful study—why couldn't she write there? *That's not what I mean,* she shouted. *It's space in my head!* It was hard being a poet with two small children underfoot. So put them in day care full-time, he told her. It made her furious when he said things like that. She already had them in day care three days a week—that was enough! She needed that time for her teaching. So don't teach, he said, *write.* She liked teaching, liked having her own money, liked getting out into the adult world. She wanted *him* to take care of the girls, if only on weekends. It would free her to write without feeling guilty. He tried, but it just wasn't possible. There was too much work to do, competitions to enter or finish. He needed the time on weekends more than she did.

She'd scream at him, slam doors, sleep with her back to him.

He sighs now, remembering the hurt of those years—his own and hers. He understands better now what she needed from him, and what he couldn't, or refused, to give. At the time he'd wait for her to thaw. She always did, her warmth and energy pulling her back to him within days. Over the years, however, he tired of it, wanting his home to be a place of respite and renewal. Hallie liked drama—sometimes he thought she thrived on it—but he didn't. "I do the best I can," he told her. "Every chance I have, I spend time with you and the girls. You don't understand what it takes to build a successful practice, support a family, get the kind of projects I want."

Round and round they went. After the girls went away to college, he thought it would be better. Her poetry was being published, she was teaching regularly, but her disappointment in him remained. To protect himself, he went inward, became more and more remote. He was happier staying at the office than going home. And then one day she left for Captiva, phoning him several weeks later. "I don't know if I love you anymore," she said. He drove to the office and buried himself, 24/7, in work.

For days, weeks, it went on that way. One weekend in Caddis Wood he looked at the early spring flowers coming up, gopher mounds marring the lawn, and decided it was time. He borrowed Joe Pratt's rototiller and methodically tilled up the yard. A wave of pleasure broke over him as the pockets of green tumbled and broke under the rotating blades and he smelled the new-turned earth. When he finished, he stood at the top of the hill and surveyed the ruin of his carefully tended lawn. He laughed, thinking he'd never have to spread fertilizer again, never have to mow, never have to mix another container of herbicide.

The garden took longer, for he had to dig it up by hand, uproot each shrub and flower. He disappeared into the rhythm, thought of nothing but the pull of muscles in his arms and back, the sound of metal hitting earth, brown roots ripped free and somersaulting into dirt and air.

Over the ensuing week he went through Alice's notebooks, reading the entries and studying her sketches and careful annotations of flowers and grasses. He consulted with the staff at Prairie Restorations and returned to Caddis Wood with supplies: bags of prairie grass seed mix, wildflower mixes, boxes planted with seedlings. He made one more circuit with the rototiller, and then, satisfied the earth was ready, he slowly zigzagged back and forth, scattering prairie grass seed. After raking it lightly into the soil, he broadcast the wildflower seed mixes and worked them into the soil.

He planted orange prairie lilies along the banks of the stream, red bee balm and cardinal flowers at the bottom of the hill. At the top of the hill he planted the blue flowers: blue vervain and wild lupine. The upper terraces he filled with white and yellow: yarrow, bunchflower, black-eyed Susan, golden alexanders.

When he was done planting and watering, he repainted the shed and helped Joe Pratt with the mowing. After the beavers built a dam in Spring Brook, he tore it out stick by stick. They built it again—he ripped it out. The monotonous labor blotted out his loneliness.

One night in Minneapolis, he went out with people from the office, drank too much, and drove his car into the light pole a block away from their house. Sitting in the car, his body spinning from the impact, he thanked God there had been no other car, that he'd not killed himself or anyone else. *I'm fucked,* he whispered as he backed the car away and drove it into the garage. The next morning he called in sick and fell asleep on the floor of the bedroom. When he woke, he called James Shay, the therapist he and Hallie had seen several times. "Hallie's gone," he said. "I'm losing my mind. Can you help me?"

James Shay saw him right away and set up a number of ap-

pointments over the next few weeks. It felt good to talk to someone. Shay was a good-humored man with rock-solid common
sense. Nothing fancy or overtly psychological about him—Carl
didn't feel psychoanalyzed, which he was grateful for. They
talked about his father, his mother, his struggles with Hallie,
his work. Shay asked him questions that he couldn't answer, so
they talked about that, his inability to answer, and the next time
they met, Shay asked him the same questions again. Why didn't
he tell Hallie how hurt he was? Why did he tuck so much of
himself away, push *her* away? Why did he bury himself at work
rather than share what he was feeling? Why couldn't he give her
what she said she needed?

On warm afternoons in Wisconsin Carl lay on the daybed
on the porch, gazing into the trees. His head ached with questions and memories.

"You really think you'd have to compromise your career to
make her happy?" James Shay asked.

"To do the work I do takes an enormous amount of time and
focus. Hallie wouldn't love me if I were a mediocre architect—
believe me."

"There's a big territory between being mediocre and being
great, isn't there?"

"How do you control that? If you don't *expect* the best of yourself, if you don't strive for it, what will happen? It's who I am. I
can't do it any other way."

"You don't think a marriage takes time? Forget architecture
for a minute. What kind of *man* do you want to be, for Hallie
and your daughters?"

"I can't separate being an architect from the rest of me."

"Perhaps you should. Perhaps you should pay attention to what
you're *not* so good at."

"It may not matter, anyway. I don't think she loves me anymore."

"Do you love her?"

"Yes."

"So why don't you show her? Give her what she says she wants: your undivided attention, your presence."

He bought a round-trip ticket to Fort Myers, return date open. Told Alex and others in the office that he was taking a leave of absence, didn't know how long he'd be gone. He needed to act right away, before pride won out, before he forgot what it all meant.

Finally, the throbbing in his neck wanes and he gets up and climbs the stairs to bed. She is sleeping when he slides in next to her, her body curled so he can fit himself to her in the old way. As he pulls her close, she sighs in her sleep. He presses himself against her, gently so as not to wake her, wishing the desire back in his body.

In the morning he smells coffee brewing and freshly made banana bread and hears Hallie humming in the kitchen. Painfully, he pulls himself up, feeling resistance in the muscles and joints in his back, hips, knees. It's after eight—stupid to stay up so late and put more stress on his body.

"Want some coffee?" Hallie asks as he enters the kitchen. Without waiting for him to answer, she pours him a cup and pulls out his chair for him. A bowl of berries, another of yogurt, banana bread steaming on the platter. He's queasy but doesn't want to disappoint her so he takes a bite of banana bread. His mouth is full of cotton so he pours himself a tall glass of orange juice and drains it. The white cordless phone from their bedroom is on the table, as is the kitchen phone. She sits down across from him.

"Clare called this morning. She and Nathan have their fingers crossed that . . . well, that whatever you've got can be treated. Did Dr. Schlain's nurse *say* there is a diagnosis?"

He pours milk into his coffee. "Not exactly . . ."

"Well, if she didn't say . . ."

"They *know*, Hal."

She takes a deep breath, nods. "Clare's invited Mama to come to Captiva for a few weeks. She wants me to join them."

"When?" He can't hide the alarm in his voice. A dull pounding begins behind his eyes.

She covers his hand with her own. "I said no, honey. I'm not leaving you."

He sits up straight, annoyed with himself. Unnerved, too, at the jealousy that shot through him when she mentioned going to Captiva. She has sworn to him that she never saw Eugene again after that winter; as far as she knows, Eugene never returned to Sanibel.

"You should go. Captiva has always been a great place for you and Clare. It might be good for the three of you."

"We'll see." She hands him the front section of the newspaper and takes the second section for herself. Once she's absorbed in her reading, he holds the paper in front of him and concentrates on the lines of ink in the headlines. He reads through the front-page story several times before he knows what it is he's reading.

When the phone rings, he startles, knocking over the glass. Hallie hands him the cordless phone and picks up the other. He is glad it's Dr. Schlain and not one of the other doctors on the team. Schlain is steady and straightforward—he's obviously done this hundreds of times. You have Shy-Drager syndrome, he says, or multiple system atrophy, a progressive neurodegenerative disorder of the central and autonomic nervous system. It progresses swiftly in some patients, slowly in others. The disease has

Parkinson's-like symptoms, which explains his sluggishness in moving, the stiffening muscles, tremors in his hands. Excessive drop in blood pressure is another symptom. When the pressure drops, he faints. As soon as he hits the ground, the pressure rises and he's okay.

"No," Schlain says gently when Hallie asks. "There is no cure or remission from the disease."

Hallie has taken his free hand in hers. His mouth is parched and he looks longingly at the empty glass. He understands the words the doctor is saying, but it's as if he's talking about someone else. *Stop, already. I've heard enough.* Hallie reads his distress, or she's had enough, too, because she interrupts, asks where they can find more information about the disease, which doctor they should see in town, if they should return to the NIH. Dropping Carl's hand, she pulls a pad of paper toward her and writes. He reaches forward for the orange juice but his hand, when he tries to pour, shakes so much that he spills it. Everything's a blur—only the ticking clock, the hum of the refrigerator, the soft scratching of Hallie's pen on the page. Finally, she puts down the pen and pours the orange juice for him.

After they've hung up, they sit quietly at the table. He hears the soft, animal-like sounds of her weeping but he can't look at her. He doesn't feel sad or angry or frightened; he doesn't feel *anything*, which is weird given the fact that he's just been told he's dying and that it's going to get pretty ugly before it's over and nobody knows how long he's got—a year if he's lucky?

When the pounding in his head grows too strong to manage, he looks up and sees how pale she is, her eyes swimming. "Could you get the ibuprofen, Hal? My head . . ."

She strides quickly out of the kitchen. He tries to remember everything the doctor said but the words bounce inside his brain like balls on a tennis court. When Hallie returns, she refills his glass again and hands him the ibuprofen. He pops them in his mouth, guzzling the juice.

"Come to the couch, honey, and lie down." She helps him up and into the living room. Sitting at one end of the couch, she lays a pillow on her lap and settles his head on it. Her hands are cool on his face and forehead. Gently she kneads his temples, massages the pressure points along the crown of his head, the muscles in his neck. Just as he closes his eyes, he sees the movement across the room, knows without having to look who it is.

HALLIE

Chapter 8
Captiva (March)

Hallie stretches to touch the sunbeam on the foot of the bed and sighs with pleasure at being in Captiva again. Just as quickly, however, she plummets, thinking of Carl. Sometimes when she wakes she lingers in the space between remembering and not, wishing their life back before the diagnosis. It's March 3, the twins' birthday and the anniversary of her father's death, and, of course, her mother, the reason for her visit. She leaps up and dresses, wanting to see firsthand the effects of the hurricane.

By the time she and Clare arrived home from the airport last night, it was too dark to see anything. Now, as she peers up at the house, she sees new shingles on the roof and fresh, unbleached wood in several of the window frames. The cottage, of older construction and built low to the ground, escaped unscathed, as did the native palms and grasses in front of the house and cottage and along the walkway. Once Hallie reaches the beach, however, devastation stops her. The beautiful wall of Australian pines that lined the beach as far as the eye could see is gone. What's left are headless trunks, broken or splintered limbs, brown earth. Other homes, hit harder than her sister's, are not yet repaired.

The houses that are being restored, Clare said last night, have owners rich enough or with sufficient insurance to pay for the work necessary to rebuild. Many, however, those modest houses and cottages owned by regular people who've lived on the island for years and survived the crippling increases in property taxes, will be sold. In their place, bigger, posher homes will be built, many of them developed on speculation or as time-shares. "I've seen the drawings," Clare said. "Hacienda-type houses next to Victorian kitsch. It's horrible."

Hallie heads up the beach toward the north end of the island, a shadow in the morning fog. Once a thick, feathery mass of trees, the denuded landscape resembles the forest at Caddis Wood after the fire: sparse, blackened trunks and branches in a naked landscape. If nature has a consciousness, does it mourn the loss of its trees? Does it ache like the body does at the site of an amputated limb? It's terrible watching the toll of the disease on Carl's body, the slow, steady loss of bodily functions. When he can no longer walk or hold himself upright, will parts of his body ache in remembrance?

Clare jogs up behind her. "You should have called me to go with you."

Hallie tries to smile. "I wanted to walk all the way to the end but I don't think I'm up to it."

Clare puts an arm around her. "It's so much better than it was. People have worked very hard cleaning up, trimming the pines, replanting palms. Just *look*."

As they walk, Clare points out the new growth that Hallie overlooked earlier. Nature, impossible to hold back, bursts forth from the ruins: tufts of green sprout from the earth; from twisted, heaved-up roots and crevices of shorn trees. Hallie's grief ebbs as she takes it in, though it is hard to imagine nature's and humans' ability to restore the landscape she remembers. As they turn their attention to the shells glistening in heaps along the beach, they fall into a familiar pattern: walking slowly, eyes trained on the ground, filling their pockets and the insides of their straw hats.

"Why didn't you tell me?" Clare's expression is torn between concern and annoyance.

"In the beginning it felt too private and then it was over and Carl and I were together again and it felt wrong to talk about it."

"But you continued to write him."

"Yes." Hallie sighs. "Not that I wanted or expected anything to happen. I just . . . don't look at me like that. We were friends. I didn't want to let him go—the connection, I mean. Is that so wrong?"

Clare looks at her. "You're kidding, right?"

Hallie stamps her foot in the sand. "*Damn it,* Clare! Aren't things hard enough without you being so judgmental?"

Clare starts to reply but stops herself. After a minute she says, "I'll get us something to drink. Then we'll lay out the shells."

Clare walks into the kitchen. She is gone a long time. Hallie sits down on the deck and begins to sort the shells from her straw hat into long vertical bands: turrets in one section; pink paper cockles in another; white-and-brown checkerboards; oysters and mussels; pastel-colored scallops; channeled whelks; spiny pink-bellied chamas. When Clare returns, she places a pitcher of iced tea on the table and hands Hallie a tall, sweating glass.

Dropping onto the deck next to her, Clare empties her pockets and begins sorting the pile from her own hat. It is quiet but for the shushing waves and wind in the sea grape leaves. Hallie lays a pair of angel wings on the pearl-colored wood, careful not to break the fragile hinge. *If I break it, Carl will never get over it. If I don't, we'll make love again when I get back.* Smiling, she sits back on her ankles to survey the unbroken halves.

"I know you're hurting, Hal," Clare says.

"When you marry someone, does it mean you give up your interior life, that you have no self that belongs to you alone?"

"Of course not."

"So what's wrong with having your own private fantasies?"

"Nothing. But you have to take responsibility for them. I hear it every week in my practice: *I'm not happy. I've met somebody else.* Then boom"—she snaps her fingers—"magic, just like that. I know how seductive it is."

"Have you or Nathan . . ."

"That's not the point!" Her voice rises. "It's easy to walk away and choose the shiny new thing, and then what? Sometimes it's the right decision, but often it's a failure of will. You go for the magic, the easiness of it, and walk away from the stale or troubled marriage. Two years down the line the magic is gone, and you realize your new partner has his own share of warts, different ones to be sure, but disappointing nonetheless. So you leave that marriage behind as well. Or, because you're older, wiser, more willing to work things out, you stick with it and make it work.

"I sound like a therapist, I know. Sometimes I hate the sound of my own voice." Even as a girl, Clare was the advice giver, the one who always knew the right thing to say. "Look, there's no perfect partner and no perfect combination of people. You keep trying and growing until one of you dies. Why do people think it's otherwise?"

"But I *know* this. I stopped it—I said good-bye to Eugene. Carl and I fell in love again."

"Yes, you did. It's just that, well, people are more fragile than we think. You gave your heart to someone else while you were still married to Carl. It's a betrayal, Hal, regardless of how you spin it. I have no idea what Carl will do. He's sick and he needs you, but he's hurt."

"But I forgave *him,* all those years of soldiering on when he wasn't there, shutting me out, putting work ahead of me and the girls. If I can forgive, why can't he?"

"Because people are complicated, and life isn't fair. Carl will do what he's capable of doing."

"What if he never trusts me again? What if he dies not knowing how much I love him?"

"I don't know, Hal. I pray he doesn't."

She feels tears rising. "It was *ten years* ago."

Clare lays down a bright orange scallop shell. "For him, it might as well have happened yesterday."

"He's dying, Clare." Her voice breaks.

Clare pushes the unsorted shells out of the way and pulls Hallie next to her, their backs against the side of the house.

"Remember that night in Dublin, how stoned we were?" Clare asks.

"What made you think of that?"

"You introduced me to Carl that day, remember? Before he left on the boat to Liverpool."

"You weren't keen on us getting married."

"You hardly *knew* him. Besides which, all that stuff with his parents . . ."

"You mean his father burning to death in a car with his mistress and Carl hating him?"

"Well, *yeah.*"

"No worse than me hating my mother."

Clare nudges her. "You don't hate Mama.

"I did then." Hallie reaches over and straightens the pair of tiny angel wings. "I bet you don't even remember what day it is."

"What do you mean?" Clare asks, puzzled.

"I *knew* you'd forgotten."

Clare squints toward the sky, thinks. "God, you're right—I did forget."

"When Carl came to the hospital the next morning, Daddy was gone. I never got to say good-bye."

"Mama was already on the bus back to California."

"Let's call the girls and wish them happy birthday."

After Clare leaves for the airport to pick up their mother, Hallie prepares a salad and mixes a marinade for the chicken. It is a short walk along the beach to the cemetery, one of her favorite places on the island. Miraculously, the trees and shrubbery surrounding the cemetery were not damaged by the hurricane. It is cool and dark as she enters the narrow path sheltered by palms, papered with brown and russet leaves. She passes a torn screen lodged in a tree and is glad she wore sandals when she sees shards of glass among the leaves.

The white gate into the cemetery, unlocked as always, swings open easily. Each time she enters, she feels the pleasure of this sheltered space: gnarly sea grape trunks, stone markers streaked with sunlight, oyster-colored sand. She weaves slowly round and between the graves, looking for telltale marks of the newly buried. After completing the circuit, she sinks gratefully onto the wooden bench.

A shadow darkens her knees and she looks up to a band of pelicans soaring overhead. The black arrows they make shimmer in her memory like beads of water. At the corner of her vision a woman in a blue dress approaches the cemetery and pauses, her arm lifted in midair. Hallie blinks and plunges back in time, to her father's bedroom and, through the window, the winged shape of a black-gloved hand on the gate.

The woman entering the yard was tall, slightly stooped, her hair hidden beneath a black cap. Hallie leaned closer to the glass: something familiar in the woman's profile. She was wearing a brown wool coat and carried a canvas bag and a black leather purse. At the sight of the horseshoe-shaped clasp, Hallie sprang to her feet.

Holding her swollen, pregnant belly, she glanced at her sleeping father and at Grandma Olga slumped in the armchair beside the bed. She moved swiftly down the hallway, past the living room where Clare's brown head was bent over a book, and across the kitchen. She reached the back door at the same time as the woman, who raised her hand to knock and froze there, the two meeting through glass. Hallie swung wide the door and stepped forward so her body filled the doorway.

"What do you want?"

The woman straightened to her full height and studied her, that taking-your-measure glance that rang a chord of memory. As she narrowed her eyes, a tiny light blinked on deep within the blue. Not the lambent flame Hallie remembered, the blazing blue that could scoop up an entire room. They stood head to head, blanketed by the cold March wind that blew into the kitchen. The hand on the strap of the canvas bag was riddled with veins.

"I've come to see your father." The same lilt to her voice, the touch of brogue that had flavored all her stories.

"How did you know?"

"Jacob sent for me."

Hallie's heart skipped a beat. How was it possible? How did he know where to find her? She stepped back enough to allow Maeve into the room. Footsteps on the hallway carpet, and Clare entered the kitchen. When Maeve turned her head, Hallie saw her break into a trembling smile. Clare reached out her two hands and took hold of Maeve's smaller one. She whisked away Maeve's coat and bag and led her into the living room, where they sat side by side on the couch.

"I'm so happy you've come," Clare said.

Maeve glanced once in Hallie's direction. Hallie felt the fist in her throat, the room gone black and woolly like a caterpillar. She winced at the red-hot rays shooting from the inside of her left leg into her groin. She'd woken up with it that morning, assumed a pinched nerve until Judy, one of the hospice nurses, said it was more likely that one of the babies was resting on her sciatic nerve. Turning on her heel, Hallie limped up the hallway and into the cocoonlike quiet of her father's bedroom. Judy had just adjusted the morphine dripping through a tube into Jacob's thin chest. Grandma Olga was leaning forward in her chair, making soft mewling noises, as she did with each new assault on her son's body. Hallie helped Judy raise the head of the bed and maneuver Jacob into a comfortable sitting position.

"Could you leave us alone for a few minutes, Judy?"

As the door closed, Hallie took her father's hand, saddened by the putty color of his skin, the way his hand fit so neatly into her own.

"What's the matter, Hal?"

"She's here, Dad."

She searched his drawn face, which had become eerily handsome as the skin receded and the bones came forward. Large sable eyes like Clare's. He closed them once, with what she assumed was relief, or gladness, before returning to her.

"I sent for her."

"That's what she said. Dad, how is that possible?"

He breathed in, out. "I've always known where she was, Hal. Last week, when I knew how close things were getting, I called her."

Hallie brushed tears from her face. "How come you never told us? We could have written, could have gone to see her . . ."

"She asked me not to, Hal."

She paced back and forth alongside the bed. Grandma Olga reached out to take her hand but she pulled away. She didn't want to be angry at her father, didn't want to upset him, weak as he was, but the fact of her mother's presence in the house was shattering.

"All these years, Dad. She could have written at least, could have called." Her voice broke and she walked to the window and looked out on the snowy yard. One knock on the door and all the memories were back. The awful, yearning need. Anger roaring like a caged thing inside her.

"I wish it could be different," her father said.

She smiled wanly. "You and me both, Dad."

"You're a grown woman now, Hal. You have a husband who loves you. You're going to have a baby."

"*Two* babies."

He nodded. "Two babies."

Her grandmother was watching them, small eyes gleaming, white hair braided into its familiar knot. Hallie took the black comb from the bureau top, wet it, and ran it gently through the wispy strands across her father's pink skull. She straightened the collar on his pajama shirt, pulled the coverlet straight and folded it neatly across his belly.

"Okay?" he asked.

She nodded. Taking her grandmother's arm, she pulled her gently to her feet and led her out of the room. Her mother and Clare were deep in conversation when Hallie and Grandma Olga reached the entryway into the living room. The old woman drew in her breath sharply when she recognized Maeve.

"You can go in now," Hallie said.

A flicker of uncertainty crossed Maeve's face at the sight of Olga. Her glance slid from Olga to Hallie, then she walked purposefully round them and down the hallway toward Jacob's room. Hallie followed, pausing at the threshold. Maeve hesitated for only a second, as if she were regaining her bearings in the room, and glided swiftly toward the bed. Jacob's face hung suspended in the open space between them, so naked that Hallie grabbed the door frame to steady herself. Her mother's hair glowed in the light as she knelt down and took Jacob's hand inside hers. Reaching forward, Hallie caught hold of the doorknob and pulled the door closed.

Vinegar leaves scuttle over sand, and palm trees creak in the wind. The woman in blue kneels beside a grave at the far end of the cemetery. The marker, a rectangle of gleaming granite, is laid flat in the ground. As Hallie watches, the woman removes a whisk broom from the knapsack she's carrying and cleans the surface of the grave, paying particular attention to the grooves in the inscription. She then sweeps a careful circle around it, creating a pattern in the sand. When this is done to her satisfaction, she takes shells out of a knapsack and arranges them carefully on the stone. Hallie's vision blurs and she wipes her eyes, tearing uncontrollably.

She and Clare had made dinner and were sitting in the kitchen with their mother when Carl arrived, stomping his boots free of snow in the doorway. By that time Hallie was nauseous from the pain shooting down her leg and radiating from the small of her back. Carl must have thought it a bizarre scene: Hallie and Clare seated at the round table in Jacob Bok's kitchen with another, older woman who looked vaguely familiar, graying red hair swept up in a loose chignon.

"Go ahead, guess," Hallie said.

"Oh, Hallie, for God's sake." Clare put a hand on Maeve's shoulder. "This is Mama, Carl. She came to see Daddy."

For such a tall man, Carl had a seamless way of walking. "I'm Carl Fens, Hallie's husband."

As they shook hands, Hallie stood and moved toward the coat closet. "We're not staying. I've got to go."

"Are you all right, Hal?" Clare asked.

"Yes, no, this thing in my leg . . ."

"What's wrong with your leg?" Carl asked.

"A pinched nerve—I'm not sure. I feel awful."

Clare hurried over to the stove and ladled soup into a Tupperware container. "Here," she said to Carl. "You can eat this at home."

Maeve, who'd stood up as well, waited quietly as they readied to leave. At the door Hallie hesitated, then turned and took a few steps back into the room. "I have some things I got in Ireland that I've saved in case I ever saw you again. If you'd like, I'll send them to you."

"What things?" A crease appeared in Maeve's forehead.

"Some photos, one of your mother, and her letters to your grandmother."

"You went to Dingle?"

"Yes, I found the house and talked to your nephew. He told me I could look in a box in her room. He didn't seem to care one way or the other so I took some of the things inside."

"You were in her room?" Maeve's voice had dropped to a whisper.

Hallie nodded. "If you'd like me to send them, just leave your address with Clare."

Carl took her arm and led her to the doorway. "Kiss Daddy

good night for me," she said to Clare. Gripping Carl's sleeve, she walked out into the snowy yard. She was weeping softly as he helped her into the car and locked her seat belt for her. Always the dream had been there: her mother would come back, wanting to see them and be part of their lives. "Oh, how I've missed you," she'd say, taking Hallie and Clare in her arms. Now, there was nothing to hope for. Soon her father would be gone, too. Her shoulders heaved with sobs.

Carl held her elbow on the icy sidewalk and helped her slowly up the long stairway leading to their third-floor apartment. When they reached the top, she felt the warm rush down her legs, stared dumbfounded at the pool of water on the rug. Six hours later the twins were born, and her father died an hour after that. Her mother left on the dawn bus to San Francisco.

Seeing that the woman has gone, Hallie walks to the newly tended grave and crouches next to it. She assumed it was a recent death, but it is not: *Lucy Marie Williams, 1952–1972. There will be summer skies / There will be butterflies / We love you darling.* She walks swiftly back to the house. The beach has emptied out—families and couples having packed up their blankets and umbrellas and left for home, only the stragglers and a few walkers remaining. Lucy Marie Williams would have been twenty years old, just two years older than the twins were the winter Hallie and Carl separated. Hallie holds her daughters' faces in her mind as she lights the grill and sets the table on the deck. She swipes her face, annoyed at how easily the tears come each time she thinks of Carl. Her mother will prefer to eat outside, within view of the water. When Hallie hears Clare's car on the gravel driveway, she hurries to the door.

Even though she saw her mother ten months ago, she is taken back at how old and frail Maeve appears. She seems to have shrunk several inches as she walks slowly up the steps. Even so, she straightens to her full height when she sees Hallie. Delft blue eyes, slightly shrunken, rimmed round with wrinkles. Hallie smiles, trying to communicate her welcome. Maeve nods. Neither one reaches out to hug or embrace, but the space between them shrinks.

While Clare settles their mother in a comfortable chair on the deck, Hallie busies herself at the grill. She is anxious, as she is each time she sees her mother, her heart wrung with its own unmet need, vying with her resolution to extinguish the bad feelings from the past. When they are ready to eat, Clare pours them each a glass of white wine and leads them in a toast to the well-being of her beloved island.

Maeve plucks at her food and drinks glass after glass of water. The pallor she arrived with disappears in the softening light. They talk about the world: the growing financial crisis, Barack Obama's presidential campaign, the ongoing war in Iraq, global warming, and the likelihood of more stage four and five hurricanes. As the sun sinks toward the horizon, they fall into a comfortable silence. A flock of birds slices through the sun's shimmery, salmon-colored swath. The best times with Maeve have always been without words, as they worked across from each other at the kitchen table—Hallie doing homework, her mother folding leaflets or planning a strike with union representatives from the local bottling plant.

After Maeve goes to bed, Hallie and her sister sit for a while on the deck. They decide to let the next few days unfold naturally, not force any particular activities.

"It's so strange," Hallie says, "that she's come back into our lives, having never been a mother to us. How old is she?"

"Eighty-six."

"Do you think she wants us to take care of her?" Hallie asks.

"I don't think she's looking for our help."

"What *is* she looking for?"

The sun is gone now, the blush of its leaving staining the dove-colored sea.

"I don't know. She doesn't seem the kind of person to need to make amends," Clare says. "Maybe she just wanted to see us."

Hallie wakes to the sound of waves. It is cooler than yesterday, with a gusty wind. As she walks from the bedroom into the light-filled front room, she gazes lovingly at the well-worn furniture, books piled on the round table and along the walls. The first time she came to Captiva, the spring after Clare and Nathan had bought the house and cottage, she stayed only a few days. It was her first trip alone without the girls and she felt too guilty to remain longer. Each year thereafter, she extended the trip a day until by the time the girls were in high school, and then college, she was coming each March for two to three weeks. Time with her sister, time alone, time to sleep and read and do what she liked without having to take care of or answer to anyone.

She makes a pot of coffee and dresses warmly, layers to be stripped down as needed. Pulling one of the bleached wooden chairs to the end of the walkway, she sits with coffee mug in hand, feet tucked beneath her. The area in front of the cottage is carpeted with grasses and long, looping vines that reach like fingers onto the beach. Here and there a burst of tiny purple or orange flowers rises from the fluttering green.

The pines hum like a hive of bees, and slate-colored waves break close to shore, driven west by a fierce riptide. An older woman walks by—straw hat hanging against her back like a sombrero. Hallie nods a hello and sips her coffee. Bottle-green lights flicker in the underbelly of the waves as if a school of incandescent fish are caught inside the tumbling surf. The sun has broken through the clouds and behind her Hallie can see patches of blue sky. Four pelicans soar in a circle overhead, bank, and glide back over the lonely pines. Their bodies cast shadows that cascade through the branches in flickering beats.

A shadow falls on her, and she looks up, shielding her eyes from the sun.

"Do you mind if I sit with you awhile?" Maeve asks.

"Of course not." Hallie pulls the other chair next to hers.

Slowly Maeve lowers herself into the seat. This close, Hallie can see the blue veins in her mother's temple. She is wearing a yellow windbreaker, sweatpants, one of Clare's woven hats. They sit quietly, gazing at the unruly waves. Hallie thinks with a pang that they are the same in this way, locked on the line between earth and sky.

"Clare told me about Carl," her mother says. "I'm very sorry."

Hallie blinks. She is unprepared for such an offering from her mother. Still, she appreciates Maeve's frankness.

"It's hard." What else can she say?

"I know how much you love him," Maeve says.

"*How?* How do you know?"

Her mother's eyes in this light are startlingly blue. "You wouldn't be with him if you didn't. And I've read your poems."

"Which poems?" She's never sent her mother any of her work.

"All of them."

Hallie gazes blankly at her.

"I went to City Lights bookstore to attend a reading and picked up a magazine that had a piece on Jake Ehrlich, the lawyer who defended the bookstore after they published *Howl*. It was a landmark First Amendment case and your father and I followed it closely. One of your poems was published in the same issue. I asked the bookstore manager, who knew me, to look for your work. He sent me each of your books when they came out."

It's easy for Hallie to close her eyes and conjure her mother's voice reciting Auden and Yeats, Akhmatova and Dylan Thomas. When she's writing, reaching for just the right cadence or rhythm in a poem, she can hear the echo of those early recitations, an auditory memory imbedded deep inside the membranes of her inner ear.

"I came to a reading you did in San Francisco," Maeve says.

"Why didn't you let me know?"

"I didn't want to upset you or disrupt the reading. I just wanted to see you."

"You did?"

"Of course I did."

"Then . . ." Hallie turns to watch the parasail boat anchor farther up the beach.

"Words aren't going to do it, you know. They won't erase or make easier what's happened."

"Easier for whom?"

"For you, mostly. It's not what I'm looking for."

"Why not?"

"It isn't something you expect—ease, comfort—when you've left your children behind."

"So, you feel guilty?"

"Of course I do. I'm not a monster, Hallie. I knew what I was doing, what it would mean. I didn't leave lightly." Her words are slow, measured, as if she's weighed them a long time. "I understand what it feels like not to have a mother."

"So, how could you do it? How could you leave us?" Hallie winces at the plaintiveness in her voice.

"I had to. I didn't believe I would survive if I had stayed."

Hallie shakes her head, baffled.

Maeve sighs. "I couldn't love you and Clare the way I should have, couldn't bond. I wanted to . . ." Her voice cracks. "But then this darkness came over me after Clare's birth. I couldn't get any peace from it—night and day, nothing to look forward to." She makes a fist against herself. "I couldn't taste anything, couldn't feel. There was no light anywhere."

Hallie remembers their family trip to Alaska the spring before her break with Carl, how sad she was, unable to sleep, wanting Carl and the girls to drive off and leave her so she could weep in peace. When she talked to her doctor about it, he asked if depression ran in her family. She didn't know. "It's probably related to perimenopause," he said. "If it gets worse, we can try an antidepressant."

"We knew so little about postpartum depression then," her mother continued. "Slowly, however, it got better. The work was the only thing that offered me any peace or sense of purpose. When I realized I was pregnant again, I was terrified. I didn't want to go out, couldn't do anything but sleep. Then you were born. For a few days it was good and then the darkness descended again. When it lifted enough that I could go out, could work again, you . . . didn't know me. You cried every time I tried to hold you." Her eyes cloud over and she turns her head.

"You can imagine, a woman who can't bond with her child to begin with, and then you cry every time I come near you." She looks directly at Hallie. "You were Jacob's from the beginning."

"I was only a child . . ."

"Of course you were. I was ill. It's not an excuse, Hallie. I'm just trying to explain it."

"Did you ever get help for it?" Hallie asks.

"I've been on antidepressants for years. There are women who actually kill their children, can you imagine? I knew I had to leave, get far away from you and Clare. Jacob was a good father, and Olga was there."

"But you got better."

"Yes, I did."

"So why didn't you come back?"

Maeve sighs. She's obviously anticipated this question. "I believed you were better off without me."

"That is so lame." Hallie can't control the bitterness in her voice. "Look, I understand depression. But once you had it under control, why didn't you communicate with us or visit? You *abandoned* us." She blinks back tears.

"I understand how you feel, Hallie . . ."

"No you *don't!* You can't possibly. Your mother died in childbirth—she didn't walk out on you. Maybe your lifesaving work for others made it worth it for you, but for Clare and me and Dad, it was," she shakes her head, "terrible. It changed the rest of our lives."

Maeve speaks slowly, her words measured. "I'm not asking you to forgive me."

"What *do* you want?"

"I wanted to see you—to know who you are. To try, if possible, to explain so at least you know that it wasn't because I didn't love your father or didn't *want* to love you and Clare. I . . . just . . . couldn't. I thought it was better for me to leave rather than stay and be an unfeeling mother, someone just going through the motions. It was something wrong in *me*—not in you or Clare."

"How depressed were you?"

She sighs. *"Very."*

"Did you ever try to kill yourself?"

"Yes, twice."

"Really?"

Maeve nods.

"Did Daddy know?"

"Both times he came out to see me." Her eyes press against Hallie. "He wouldn't divorce me. He wanted me to have medical benefits and . . . he loved me. We loved each other."

Hallie remembers the rare trips her father took. He hardly ever traveled, once a year for a law conference and then a few trips to see an old friend in California.

"Does Clare know all of this?"

"During her last visit I talked to her. I asked her not to tell you, told her I would do so myself."

Hallie sighs, years of sorrow weighing on her. Why didn't her father tell them about Maeve's depression? Wasn't it important information for them to have? "So much time holding on to this terrible hate and grief. I mean, hating your mother! What kind of person hates her own mother? And then, the fear, when I was pregnant myself, that I wouldn't be able to love my children. If you aren't mothered yourself, can you mother a child?"

Hallie leans forward in her chair, rocking slightly. "Clare and I have spent so much of our lives in opposition to you. We were determined not to be like you, not to walk away from things. For me, of course, it was the work that took you away. Your need to be of use, to do good, to save people in need. Better them than your own family. I made sure I didn't work too hard, that I was home with the girls. I resented Carl because he worked all the time, believing he loved the work more than me. Oh, it makes me so sad." She bows her head onto her knees and weeps.

"Your family came first for you," Maeve says. "You never

wavered in it. Just as you never wavered in your love of poetry. What child loves E. E. Cummings and Emily Dickinson more than any fairy tale? You were a fierce little girl, Hallie. You're a fierce woman. Your father would be proud of you."

Hallie makes no effort to wipe away her tears. Behind them the wind blows through the fringed branches of the two remaining Australian pines. The air is thick with pelicans, and seagulls cluster at the edge of the water. Walkers pass, some bending and scooping for shells. An older woman in a kayak, beyond the waves, skates across the iridescent water.

"I couldn't send you the things of your mother's, the things I brought from Ireland."

Maeve looks at her quizzically.

"The night Daddy died . . . I said I'd send them to you but you didn't leave your address."

Maeve nods, remembering. "I thought that whatever you found should stay with you."

"They belong to you. I want you to have them." Hallie rises from the chair and goes into the cottage, returning with a small wooden box, which she sets in her mother's lap. Clare has arrived and is sitting on the other side of their mother. Maeve runs her hand over the worn lid before opening it. A sheaf of papers tied with string, several black-and-white photographs and holy cards. She turns over one of the photos, a wedding picture—on the back the date, 1898, and the names Nualla and Griffin Byrne.

"These are your grandparents," Hallie says. "Your cousin, Sean Byrne, said Nualla died in 1954. His father, Donal, was your uncle."

"What was he like?"

"He was nice enough. I told him what I knew, that your mother had died of childbirth fever in a hospital in Chicago. He said the family never knew there'd been a baby."

Maeve nods and looks closely at another photo, marred by a brown crease down its middle. A tall, willowy girl leans against a rock wall with her hands folded across her chest. She is wearing a hat, but a lock of hair has come loose and blown out and away from her face. The notation reads, *Our Kathleen, April 21, 1923.* Slowly Maeve unwraps the string and sorts through the papers and cards.

The first letter is addressed to Nualla with a Chicago postmark. Hallie knows the letters by heart. News of the crossing, Ellis Island, the train to Chicago. Nualla's other brother, Emmett, gave Kathleen a room in his house. Bad plumbing and poor ventilation but a grand view. Her mother's lessons in sewing had been of use, for she had a job as a stitcher in a factory that made boys' caps. Her aunt and uncle were part of a group organizing for a union. Such smart people with their brave ideas.

The next folded slip of yellowed paper was a typed note signed by a Sister Cornelius of Cook County Hospital informing Nualla that her daughter Kathleen had died of pneumonia on May 7, 1924. No details, no documents, no mention of a baby.

"Did your father ever talk about her?" Clare asks.

Maeve shakes her head. "He said she was pretty and shy and worked as a stitcher in a factory. She put his name on the birth certificate so when she died, they called him."

"Was he good to you?" Clare asks.

"Good enough. He never married so it was just me and him. He was head of the local laundry drivers' union so he took me with him on his rounds—on Saturdays we went to the meeting hall. I'd do my homework at a little table and play hopscotch on the sidewalk until he was done."

"Who took care of you after he died?" Hallie asks.

"I was eighteen. I used the life insurance policy to go to college. That's where I met your father."

Hallie sighs, sadness washing over her. Suddenly, all three of them become aware of an agitation in the air and water. Dozens of pelicans, more than Hallie has ever seen, are diving headfirst into the sea. When they surface, their beaks shimmer with silver, wiggling meat that is swallowed whole or spilled into the sea. Gluttonous gulls fight over the leftovers. A group of scarlet ibises land next to a crane, red legs aglow in the sunlight, and poke their long saffron beaks doggedly into the sand. The water shivers and pops as if charged with electric current.

"What's going on?" Hallie asks her sister.

The two of them get up and walk to the water's edge, where they peer into pockets black with teeming fish. Sanderlings, terns, and sandpipers mill around their feet and up and down the beach. The crane waits patiently for fish that get away. Beyond the moving minnows, a manta ray leaps out of the water like a gigantic bat.

"Good lord," Hallie whispers. Her mother has joined them and the three stand mesmerized by the sight. The air is raucous with quarks and caws.

"Have you ever seen it like this?" Hallie asks.

"Not really," Clare says. "Though things have been weird ever since the hurricane."

"It will all be gone if Washington doesn't do something," Maeve says grimly.

"Oh, Mama," Clare moans. "Don't say that."

"Well, it's true," Maeve says. "Nature is moving close to the brink and all those people can talk about are terrorism and taxes. *They* are the terrorists, destroying our earth with their greed and denial, creating a breeding ground in Iraq and Afghanistan for every disenfranchised lunatic wanting revenge on the West. I know you love it here, Clare, but it may not last."

"On that cheery note, I think we should go inside for breakfast." Hallie takes her mother's arm. Maeve leans against her as they make their way up the path.

The three of them fall into an easy rhythm. Hallie and Clare resume their familiar patterns: morning coffee on the deck, a walk on the beach, then long blocks of individual time as Hallie retreats to the cottage to read and write and Clare does her e-mail correspondence and continues work on a new article. Maeve, who wakes later, waits for Clare to finish at the computer and reads the day's news online. She then joins one or both of them for a short walk. Much of her day is spent reading and dozing in the chaise longue on the deck or sitting on the wooden chair gazing out to sea.

Late in the afternoon Hallie and Clare put on their bathing suits and take their chairs onto the beach. They set up the umbrella for Maeve, who sits in the shade while they read in their chairs or nap on the blanket. When it's hot enough, they swim. Clare dives in headfirst while Hallie takes her time, inching forward to get her body acclimated to the temperature of the water. When they were children, Clare would splash her and Hallie would scream obscenities. Now, Clare waits until Hallie has finally immersed and then they swim or bodysurf into shore. Sometimes they float, rocked by the gently rolling waves.

Each evening they come together to prepare and eat a meal, drink wine, and talk. For the first few days they talk mostly of national and international news or politics. Maeve seems content to stay on the periphery of their lives. She doesn't interrupt or intrude, voices her opinion if she is asked or when they are discussing world events. As the week progresses, however, she begins to ask them questions about their lives—their husbands,

Cordelia and Beatrice, Hallie's work reviewing books and teaching, Clare's practice and research.

"What are you working on?" Maeve asks one evening, gesturing with her thin hand at the porch in the cottage below where Hallie's laptop and notebooks are visible on the table.

"She's working on a book of poems about Demeter and Persephone," Clare says. "Actually, this is the *second* book she's written. But this time she's got it—I'm sure of it."

"What happened to the first book?" Maeve asks.

"You want to tell her or should I?" Hallie wonders how much wine her sister has consumed.

Clare waves blithely at her. "No, no, you tell her. It's *your* book."

Since her first reading of the myth when she was a teenager, Hallie's thought of the story as peculiarly hers. Then, she found comfort in Demeter as the loving mother, who, besotted with grief over her daughter's disappearance, scoured the earth until she found her and then ravaged nature in punishment. She empathized with Persephone, the frightened child needing her mother to save her.

Twenty years later she began a book of poems. She filled bookshelves and file drawers with research, read every version of the myth she could find. She wanted to create her own version of it, manage the story with rhyme and meter the way poets like Sylvia Plath and Louise Bogan had done.

"So, what was your version?" Maeve asks.

Before she can answer, Clare says, "Her Demeter was a narcissist who raised her daughter dutifully but without love."

Hallie glares at her.

"Well, it's true," Clare says. "How can you love a child when you love yourself best of all? Demeter goes to the underworld to reclaim her title as queen, to reclaim, too, her brother and former lover. Persephone is this ferocious teenager—angry, rebellious, desperate to be free. Going to the underworld with Hades is her ticket out. Better still, she gets to spite the mother who abandoned her."

"I'm not sure I'd put it quite that way," Hallie says, looking pointedly at her sister. "My editor hated the book."

"Why?" Maeve asks.

"She said the poems were technically fine but there was 'no air' in them. They were completely self-conscious. And she didn't like the overall vision."

"Because it was controversial?"

"Because she *perverted* it," Clare says. "She made Demeter a monster. Any daughter would run for the hills with a mother like that."

Hallie leans over and snatches the wine glass from Clare's hand. Annoying as she is, Clare always saw the truth in what Hallie had done with the story. *When you quit seeing Demeter as Mama, you'll write a better book.*

"It was how I saw things then," Hallie says to Maeve.

Her mother nods. "And now?"

"After Bea's accident," Hallie says, "Carl and I would take turns sitting with her. I wondered what it was like to be locked inside a coma. Could she hear us? Could she feel anything? I was glad she was so fearless, you know, so unafraid of the dark. She'd passed over into this other world, and I was the one left behind. It was the same after Tim died. *Cordelia* was the one being pulled into hell and I couldn't do anything to stop it."

"So you wrote another book," Maeve says.

"I'm writing it."

"Would you read me some of it?"

Hallie feels a sudden rush of tears and turns her head away. It is all too much, suddenly, these collisions between past and present, reality and myth.

"Of course she will," Clare says.

Hallie is restless during the night, unsettled by dreams, and wakes tired and fretful. She reaches for her notebook and writes what she remembers: Demeter pacing the perimeter of the cave, a young woman lying on a gurney in a hospital corridor, a vacant hospital bed with Carl's name on the door. After her father died, she had dreams in which she could feel his presence, knew he was there in the next room but she could never reach him, never make contact. Each time she arrived at the place where he was, he was gone. Will it be that way after Carl dies, will he be absent even in her dreams?

Abandoning sleep, she decides to walk to the north end of the island. She puts the notebook from that spring in 1996 in her day pack and leaves a note for Clare. In the past she and Clare would make this trek several times a week and then, the year of the first dredging operation to prevent further beach erosion, she and Clare walked to the point every day to be out of hearing of the machinery. When Carl followed her to Captiva, she took him there. It hurts that this place that is so special to her bore the brunt of the hurricane. She wants to see it up close and honor its losses, the way she felt when she flew to New York City with Carl after 9/11.

The past few days she's felt a soreness in her chest, like a bruise or a pulled muscle—sadness over her mother, grief for Carl and the distance still between them. As she advances down the beach, she feels each infinitesimal grain of salt and sand against her face, as if her skin has dissolved and it is all nerve endings beneath.

The destruction intensifies the farther she walks. Almost every house has sustained damage: roofs lifted off, shingles torn away, screens shredded or left swinging from nearby trees, decks sheared off, soffits twisted. The air rings with the sound of chain saws and hammers, but many homes stand in wait, wrapped in blue sheeting. There are too many, Clare says. Either the insurance hasn't been sorted out or there aren't enough workers to keep up with it.

The damage to nature is heartbreaking. Huge piles of limbs and branches rise in the clearings between houses. Clare warned her that the South Sea Islands Resort at the end of the island, and North Island across from it, took a direct hit. The resort is closed indefinitely, buildings boarded up or covered in plastic. When she reaches the breakwater at the farthest end, she peers across to North Island, where the hurricane eye wall came ashore. The storm cut a channel through the heart of the island, severing it in half. The view is haunting: trees downed or lopped off at the knees, roots upended in massive, labyrinthine tangles. These trees, Clare says, are mangroves and won't grow back. Wind and waves have buried the sea grass beds there, destroying habitat for manatees. Hallie wonders how many other birds and animals have been displaced as well.

At the northwestern point she spreads her towel on a narrow spit of land sheltered by a causeway to her right and a rock wall behind her. Standing knee deep in the Gulf, she scans the shells tumbling through her parted feet. Her eyes are trained to screen the detritus for a color or shape just right or big enough to be worth something. After finding a few beauties, Hallie curls up on the towel and removes her journal from that spring in 1996.

The weeks after she left Carl take wing in her memory. She was plagued with a kind of vertigo, dizziness that came and went.

It entered the long immigrant poem she was writing, echoing the seasickness and disjunction her characters felt. The voices in the poem traveled with her when she slept. She'd wake nauseous, roll with giddiness when she stood up from her desk. She debated asking Eugene about it, but what would she say—that each time he kissed her the air shattered, hundreds of blue shards, in each one the face of her husband? It was why she ended their relationship, realizing how deeply she was bound to her marriage.

She was still reeling when she returned from her walk that day and saw Carl sitting on the steps leading to Clare's house. He didn't see her right away—he was looking in the other direction, the sun bright overhead—so she had a clear view of him. His hair, streaked with gray, was longer than usual, raked back from his face. Without her there to remind him, he hadn't thought about a haircut. He was wearing jeans and a T-shirt, a pair of running shoes. He looked younger, more himself without his usual office clothes.

She plunged, losing the air, the ground beneath her feet. If it weren't for the wooden chair pushed onto the beach, she would have fallen. Maybe it was the angle, the unexpectedness of seeing him in this place she'd come to inhabit over the past weeks, or the image that came swiftly and vividly to mind of him sitting on the stairs in the house where she was living in Oxford. When he saw her, he stood up quickly, just as he'd done that day. The long unfolding of his body, the way he reached up his hand to push back his hair, a look of wary expectation on his face. In her mind she moved forward, wanting to put her arms around him, but her body stood still, hat gripped in her hand. He, too, stood as if frozen, hands at his sides. She motioned to the chairs on the walkway and they sat.

"You look tired," she said.

He nodded.

"How long are you here for?"

"As long as I want."

"What about your projects, the office . . ."

"I told them I was taking some time off. There's nothing Alex and the staff can't handle for the time being."

In all the years they'd been married, he'd never taken off more than two weeks for a family vacation. When the twins were born, and after Bea's accident, he'd managed to continue working—going in at odd hours, splitting his time between the office and home. She bent down and plucked a shell from between her toes.

"You want to see the house?" she asked.

"Sure."

Hallie's eyes tear as she reads the pages from that time, some of them written then, some later. When she showed him the cottage, he was chastened by how unlike their home it was. For years they'd argued over her sense of style and his, until she gave up, letting him make the decisions. He, after all, was the architect, the one who knew more, knew best. Colors, furniture, art, arrangement mattered to him in a way she simply could not understand. Only when they bought the cabin in Wisconsin did he step back, not objecting when she filled it with furniture belonging to Alice or taken from her father's house, found objects from her walks with the girls, artwork she chose herself.

Here, Clare told her to make the cottage her own. She painted the rooms, bought a set of wicker furniture, refinished an old oak table and chairs. The shelves were filled with framed photographs, books, plants, plates brimming with shells. Photos and quotes written on colored index cards covered the refrigerator. It was a warm, cozy space where she felt completely happy and at home.

The first few nights Carl stayed in the guest room in Clare's house. He was nervous with her, tentative. He took in the decor of the cottage as if he were learning something about her for the first time. It was the same for her when she showed her his sketches, talked about his projects or what he was reading. As if it were all new and interesting with no need for judgment.

Clare returned to Seattle to give them privacy and space. Carl slipped seamlessly into Hallie's simple routines. Each morning he went for long runs up the beach; she was happy to see him jogging again. When he returned, they made breakfast together in Clare's kitchen and ate on the deck. She took him to the chapel, the cemetery, the pink-and-white gingerbread house she fantasized owning someday. Each day they drank wine on the beach at sunset.

The second week they walked here, to the end of the island. The spring break travelers all had returned home and the beach was empty, no one about. As she unpacked their lunch, she realized the world was stationary, the awful vertigo gone. They swam. He sketched while she read. She crept next to him and slept, feeling the drumming of his heart. When she woke he was lying on his side looking at her. She felt the irresistible pull of his desire and rolled toward him, fitting her body to his. His body had always spoken for him and she was grateful for it, wondering why she put such emphasis on words. They made love fast and then again, slowly, the way they had hundreds of times before, only different.

Hallie closes her eyes and listens to the sound of wind, waves shushing against sand. She fell in love twice that spring. One man was all fever and the other's fever had come and gone and come again. *But I never really loved Eugene, did I?* How could she, knowing him only a few weeks? The flaws in him as yet undiscovered, no chance to disappoint or let her down, a man not yet needing forgiveness. She leans down and plucks a pair of angel wings from the sand. As she brushes the sand away, the wings break open in her hand. Trying not to weep, she tucks the tiny shells into her notebook and packs up to return home.

Her heart aches as she gazes at the poor severed halves of North Island. "You know what you've lost, don't you?" she says aloud. "What it felt like to be whole and what it's like now that part of you is gone." With time, nature might rebuild the channel cutting the island in two, but life here would never be the same, not for the residents, the wildlife, the eternal, changing waters of the Gulf.

CARL

Chapter 9
Caddis Wood (July)

Carl leans sideways, his weight on the hoe, and breathes in the pungent smell of newly turned earth. It never wanes, this pitch of the senses as a new garden takes root. The planting took longer than usual this year, his stamina low, the heat hard for him to bear. But now he feasts on the new growth, happily peruses the circular garden inside the rectangular fence line latticed with morning glories and trumpet vine. Lettuce just up in the middle; the surrounding quadrants filled with tomatoes, beans, eggplant, rhubarb; the outer rim with its carrots, peas, its perfect rows of corn. Out of the corner of his eye, a shadow cast.

He hurls the hoe into the soil and chops feverishly. "Don't think you're going to change anything, old man." *Old man,* he thinks. *He's younger than I am.*

A hand on his arm startles him. "You ready for our hike, Dad?"

"Oh, I didn't see you, Cory."

"Sure you feel up to it?" She plucks his hat from the fence post and sets it on his head.

"Absolutely. If I have to go, I'll pee under a tree."

"That's the spirit. Who were you talking to?"

Carl lays down his hoe and opens the gate. "Old unfaithful

there." He jerks his thumb toward the sundial. *"Him."* Cordelia peers across the black soil, rows of erupting shoots, to the empty copse of pines beyond the fence.

"You're too much the scientist, Cory. If you'd become a Catholic, at least you'd have had some belief in the invisible world."

"The *invisible* world?"

"Just because you can't see someone doesn't mean he isn't there."

"*Who* isn't there?"

"You can quit looking at me like that, as if I'm playing tiddly-winks. The doctors say my brain's perfectly fine. Whatever else goes, at least I'll know it."

She bites her lip. *Lighten up,* he wants to say. *It's not your body deteriorating like a rotting vegetable.* Her face chastens him.

"I'll tell you when I get it sorted out. It's still a mystery to me, so if I start pontificating about it—who he is, what he's doing here sort of thing—you'll think I've gone off the deep end. Which I haven't, I promise you."

"Okay, so . . ." She fumbles, then brightens. "Let's talk about the project."

"What about it?"

She cuffs him lightly. "I've settled on the plants we're going to use: water lettuce, water hyacinth, duckweed."

"And the dry ones?"

"Sunflower, rapeseed, Indian mustard, blue sheep fescue."

"And poplar."

"Of course, poplar." She pulls from her pocket a folded piece of graph paper on which she's drawn a table that shows the metals and other toxins each plant will be responsible for.

He can't help but marvel at the beauty of it: native plants that suck up metals and other toxins through the roots and transport them via stems and leaves into cellular compartments where they are stored and then either converted into less toxic compounds or transformed into vapor. All along the way the plants send out waves of antioxidant compounds that protect the cell's interior from damage. *Hyperaccumulator* plants, a totally new concept to him but one well known to Cordelia and the other botanists.

"It's amazing they can survive with so much poison in their system," he says.

"And some people think botany is boring."

He is eager to show her the latest version of the floating, web-like structure he has designed to cover a portion of the dump. Her hyperaccumulator plants will sit just beneath the surface, their free-flowing roots acting as tiny vacuum cleaner hoses to leach toxins out of the water.

"It's hard to believe, looking at the site, what a ruin it is," she says. "You've got this beautiful, totally natural-looking surface rooted, literally, in poison."

"Yes, but we're going to restore it. Don't look at me that way—the job for you and your team is to help us figure out how to bring the land itself back to life and protect what's left."

"What am I, Jesus?"

"I thought you didn't believe in Jesus."

She grins. "It could take upwards of twenty years to remediate the site using only hyperaccumulator plants."

"Which is why we've got a dozen consultants and engineers working with us. The plants just happen to be my personal favorite."

"Mine, too." She takes his arm. "Now that I've got you back in the *visible* world, why don't we get going."

They wend their way along the curving garden path and onto the stone bridge where he halts, a sinking feeling in his stomach.

"It's not wide enough for a wheelchair," he says.

Cordelia squints at him. "So, we'll build another bridge."

He surveys the stream, the banks, the sloping meadow. "Where?"

"I don't know, *anywhere*. Right next to it if we have to."

He shakes his head. "It would ruin it."

"Dad, it's *your* bridge. Tear this one out and replace it with one you can get across in a wheelchair."

He grips the warm stone in his right hand, loving its hardness, the way the sun bakes the rough surface, turning it innumerable colors. When he designed the bridge, he focused on the form, the stone, its connection to land and stream. He never once thought he'd get too old, or sick, to cross it.

She follows a few steps behind him as he crosses the meadow. Simultaneously their hands reach out to brush the feathery tips of little bluestem. He spots an Edwards' hairstreak and an Appalachian brown butterfly weaving between purple stalks of prairie clover. *Cordelia*, he mouths, pointing, but her quick eyes have spotted them. The bird feeder spins with competing goldfinches, but Hallie, her head bowed over the table, doesn't look up—either at the birds or at him and Cordelia. The hum of the sewing machine, busy since early morning, heightens the clamor of insects. Hallie's taken down all the curtains in the white cabin, torn them into rags, and is sewing new ones. For the past two weeks it's been one task like this after another: new covers for the couch cushions, a refinished table, more bookshelves.

He grabs a walking stick he fashioned for himself several years ago, using it as a tool to clear the trails of fallen branches or ward off a curious snake. Without conferring, he and Cordelia head for the car. If they walk to Echo Pond from here, he will tire too quickly. She gets behind the wheel of Hallie's Prius and drives toward the McGaugheys', parking just past the turnoff to

Lucas and Livy's house at the beginning of the summer road. The road would be easier on him, but he turns onto the forest path and she follows happily. He wonders if she's remembering, as he is, the dozens of times they have traversed this trail. Livy's red plastic markers flutter wanly, and he makes a note to have Joe or Marnie replace them before they deteriorate completely.

He slows on the ascent to Echo Pond, and she waits patiently for him to catch up. On the ridge overlooking the pond he sits gratefully on Henry Badenhope's bench and rubs his aching neck.

"I'll be back in a minute," Cory says and heads back across the trail.

He closes his eyes and feels the beating sun even in the shade. Maybe it's the blood coursing through his veins, letting him know he's still alive. How foolish he'd been to think he could hold off the inevitable, that the absence of a definitive diagnosis meant there was hope that these debilitating symptoms were an explainable fluke, having to do with advancing age perhaps, a tenacious virus that would disappear without a trace. *It's the Doppler effect,* he thinks, *when the sound of something coming at you has a higher pitch than the sound of the same thing moving away.* For him, however, it's the opposite, for the sound of his approaching life consists primarily of the events he's already lived.

He hears the hum of crickets, lap of water, shushing leaves. Cordelia must have gone down into the wetland. During their first summer here, before they'd conceived the twins, he and Hallie had searched the wetland for showy lady's slippers. Lucas told them where to look, marked the spots on a map, but they couldn't find them. The summer after the twins were born, there was no time to explore together. He continued to search, hating the tired, caged look on Hallie's face each time he returned from a hike or a fishing expedition, the smell of earth and water on his clothes. She couldn't leave the cabin for more than thirty minutes, so much milk in her breasts, the sound of the babies always in her ears.

He didn't tell her he'd found the lady's slippers when, in that second summer, he led Hallie down the hill from Echo Pond and into the marshy thicket full of ferns and huge, primeval skunk cabbage. When she spotted the lady's slippers, green spearlike stems and white petals outlined in a shaft of sunlight, she cried out joyously. He pretended it was she who'd found them, sank to his knees next to her on the mucky ground, and brushed the tiny rose-colored pouches with his fingertips. He was grateful for the unveiled happiness on her face, the reemergence of that small but essential part of her that had been cut off from him since the twins were born.

"You feel up to hiking over to Osprey?" Cordelia says, startling him.

He looks up at her. In all the time she's spent here since the fire, to his knowledge she's not returned to the parts that burned. *He* has—he's kept close watch on the regrowth, marveled at the emerging beauty of the charred landscape.

"Cory, are you sure . . ."

"Dad." She pauses to gather herself. He sees in her face the teenager who rebelled against rules that made no sense to her, who refused to be thwarted when she wanted something badly enough, like Tim McGaughey, whom he and Hallie loved but didn't want for her, not in *that* way, at least, the two of them fast friends since childhood and a couple in their teens. The romance happened right before his eyes, caught him unaware like a sudden summer storm. Both sets of parents had been watching, warning each other against it. The kids were too close—

they should branch out, date other people. It was like talking to
the moon. "He's my soul mate," Cordelia said. "We were born to
be together."

"I want to see it."

"Okay, let's go."

She walks ahead of him, kicking loose twigs from the path
and holding back the overhanging branches. The narrow trail
is harder to navigate than he remembers, and he leans heavily on his walking stick for balance. As they near the meadow,
and the part of the forest that burned, he conjures the smell of
smoke and, farther back, the resin of newly planed wood. The
sawhorses stood that day on the grass between the summer cabin
and the skeleton of the new house. Heat lightning crackled in
the pallid, stuffy air. It was early, not yet nine, and he and Tim
had been working since seven, trying to beat the heat.

Tim and Cordelia had arrived three weeks earlier from
California, taking their first extended vacation since starting
graduate school. Tim had received his master's degree in forestry
two years before, and was working for the Forest Service. Cory
had just graduated from Berkeley with a Ph.D. in botany and
would start a teaching and research fellowship in September.
They were eager to help with the new house, even in the oppres-
sive heat.

The drought was in its second year and there was scarcely a
breeze in the dry, parched forest. Containment was mandatory
everywhere; no longer could a fire—especially anywhere near
homes—be allowed to burn itself out. In western Wisconsin, as
elsewhere, the Forest Service had trained a large force of men
and women, many of them as young as seventeen, as volunteer
firefighters. The whole area was on Level Five alert. There were
bans on all burning—even grills were forbidden. Every member

of Caddis Wood had extra hoses and water barrels ready to hose down buildings and trees.

"It's a textbook case for fire," Tim said the day after they arrived. "This late in the season most trees and foliage have stopped growing and are beginning to go into dormancy. Same for the grasses. There's nothing you might normally count on as a heat sink or fuel break. Everything's simply too dry. All you need is one spark and the whole forest will explode."

Carl hears Cordelia's intake of breath as they approach the wedgelike opening in the green landscape and the first view of partially burned trees. The periphery is a patchwork of living and dead trees: some lying lifeless on the ground, others broken and shorn of green, a few scorched on one side and untouched on the other. As they advance and the burn intensifies, a strange beauty emerges. Where the fire burned strongest, the trees are an army of armless, blackened snags as far as the eye can see. No longer cushioned by curtains of green, they seem small in number, their stark spines backlit by blue sky. The forest floor, however, is a riot of new growth and color: pink-petaled fireweed, large-leaved asters, ferns and bracken, wild geraniums, pin cherries, dozens of new saplings.

He takes her arm and points. "See the growth at the top? They've already reseeded."

The best they could figure was that a bolt of lightning had hit a dead snag in the woods south of Echo Pond. If the wind had been blowing north, the pond might have stopped the fire or slowed it down. What everyone imagined started out as a simple spot fire soon swelled into leaping fire swirls that spread wildly through dead needles, leaves, grasses, and twigs.

"Tim was with you and Lucas, right?" Cordelia says.

"Yes."

They exit the path onto a sandy plateau overlooking Osprey Meadow. Every few years the beavers build a dam on the northern edge, and the low-lying swale fills with water. Carl can remember summers when the water was so high that ospreys nested in the branches of drowned trees. It was dry, however, for several years before the fire and has stayed so ever since. The drought shrank the narrow stream running through it and baked the grasses and sedges into dry tinder.

"Mom and I were sleeping when the alarm went off. It was so hot the night before that Tim and I went down to the stream and jumped in to cool off."

Joe Pratt sounded the alarm a little after nine. By the time the Caddis Wood men met up with the Clam Falls volunteer fire crew on the summer road, the fire had soared skyward, igniting the living and dead needles and twigs and jumping from treetop to treetop. The group split up, half heading to the northwest and Osprey Meadow, and the rest spreading out to dig a fire line to try to stop the fire burning to the southeast. A team from the Forest Service at Spooner joined them at Beaver Lodge Lake.

It was backbreaking work, he remembers, especially in the intense heat. Men with chain saws were at either end of the line. They cut everything high along their path: shrubs, trees, low-hanging branches. He, Lucas, and several others followed, pulling the brush out of the way and throwing it outside the line. Tim and a few men trailed behind with axes and Pulaskis, chopping and removing small shrubs and roots. Next came men and boys with shovels who dug and widened the trench.

Carl wobbles and almost falls as they descend the slope into the meadow. The grass is waist high and thick, the hummocky ground making it hard to walk, but Cordelia heads resolutely for the deer stand in the middle of the meadow. He shakes his head and remembers the three of them—Cory, Bea, and Tim—dancing on a stage bedecked with multicolored streamers.

"Didn't you guys bring a boom box out here once?"

She smiles. "It was Tim's idea. We dressed up like hippies and played your old Woodstock tape, pretending we were at a rock concert."

She reaches the stand first, climbs on, and drops her hand to help him up. It's awkward and takes a while, as his legs have gone wooden and won't cooperate. He sits against the sun-baked rail and drinks from Cordelia's water bottle. Through the slats the meadow is a sea of rippling green. He listens to the wind, the gently clapping popple leaves.

"How much do you remember?" She stands next to him, her hand on the rail.

"Everything." For a long time he couldn't get the details of that day out of his head: the whooshing, popping noise—the horrific heat—cones and trees exploding from the heat of their own resin—smoke—ashes and soot and trees reduced to black poles—pinwheels of fire.

They were working as hard as they could to get ahead of it, forcing their arms and legs to move, and then somebody said the wind had shifted and the group making the firebreak along the east edge of Osprey Meadow needed help. Tim said there'd be trouble there, and left.

"Lucas wanted them to stay together, but Tim said there were boys in that other group and nobody with any real experience fighting a fire. The guys from the Forest Service knew how fast it would travel once it hit the dry grass, and they were worried the boys from Clam Falls would put themselves in jeopardy, which is exactly what happened."

Cordelia nods, her eyes moving with the rolling grass.

Mike and Joe Holman were sixteen and seventeen, with some volunteer fire training but nothing like what was needed for a fire like that. None of the boys and men in the Clam Falls group had ever been in a fire before. The first ball of fire jumped over the break at the northern end, and within minutes, one spot fire after another ignited in the grass. The wind had shifted, and fire was rocking and catapulting in all directions.

The roar and heat of the fire behind them and the speed of the spot fires must have sent a terrible fear through the group. Dennis McGhee, the chief of the Spooner crew, caught a few of them racing away and directed them over to Beaver Lake Lodge to the east. Tim was already at the meadow by then, trying to calm the Holman boys and direct them away from Osprey. Suddenly, Mike Holman must have panicked, for he dropped his shovel and sprinted into the meadow. His brother Joe hollered after him, but the noise of the fire was deafening. So Joe started after Mike. Tim grabbed Joe's shirt, yelling at him to stop, but he broke free and then Tim started running, too, dropping his ax behind him on the grass.

"He must have thought he could catch them in time and lead them off to the east," Carl says. Cordelia rocks back and forth on the deer stand, as if following the boys' course through the meadow.

The last anyone saw, Mike was almost to the middle of the meadow, Joe about twenty yards behind him, with Tim about ten yards south of Joe. The location of the Holman boys' bodies suggested that the fire overran them pretty quickly. Tim veered toward the south and Lost Creek.

"If he'd been working a crew in California," Cordelia says, "he would have been wearing his fire suit and had his shelter." She leans down to help him up. "Let's go."

He climbs awkwardly down from the stand, and she steers him across the other side of the meadow and onto the path toward Beaver Lodge Lake. With the overgrown shrubbery, the old path is hard to find. The deer, whose primordial instinct goes beyond memory or reason, have made a new path. She spots it and leads him forward. He's hurting now, his legs sore, neck on fire, but he's not going to stop. If he faints, she knows to wait a few minutes and he'll get right up.

"I've got to pee," he says. She moves away to give him privacy. He wonders what it will be like six months from now, if she'll have to help Hallie take care of him. It chills him to think he'll need to be dressed by others, cared for like a child.

They continue forward through the scarred woods. It's hard getting his bearings as they follow the deer path, his memory dependent on the original landscape. The farther they travel from the meadow, the area of the most intense burn, patches of burn appear. Deeper in the woods, the fire destroyed the understory and trees with low-hanging branches. Thicker-barked trees were singed but are still alive, as are most of the bigger pines.

When they reach Lost Creek, he stops and struggles to catch his breath, gripped by the memory of that day. Not just finding Tim but being here with Lucas, his old and dear friend, who was seeing something no father should ever have to see. Cordelia puts her arm around him.

"Tell me, Dad."

He leans hard against the walking stick. "One of the men from the Forest Service got here first and radioed back for them to send Lucas. They knew he was a doctor. Lucas was running so fast I could hardly keep up. When we got here, Tim was sitting in the creek, his back up against the trunk of that red pine." He points, grabs Cordelia's shoulder to steady himself.

He wants to expunge the images from his memory. Tim's

shoes and pants had been burned off and his feet were gone, only charred clubs left. To this day he cannot understand how Tim made it as far as he did. Skin hung in patches from his legs, arms, and chest. He was in terrible pain when they arrived, but when he saw Lucas, his face changed. Relief at first and then a kind of concern, as if he were trying to protect them.

"Tim was scooping water into his hat and drinking. I knelt beside him to help but Lucas told me to stop, that it would make him sick. Lucas was beside himself for not having anything with him he could give Tim. We took off our shirts and Lucas wrapped one around Tim's feet and the other around his chest because he was shivering. Tim kept asking for water and Lucas gave in, and Tim drank so much he vomited. He kept asking us if Mike and Joe had made it. I didn't have the heart to tell him they were gone.

"Dennis McGhee and another man got there with a stretcher, and they helped us carry Tim through the woods. One of the trucks met us on the logging road."

"It was just luck that we were at McGaugheys' cabin," Cordelia says.

He nods, remembering, the three women racing to the truck and peering into the back, where he was sitting with Tim. Lucas raced into the house for his medical bag. Livy cried out and put her hands up to her face. Cordelia pushed past her, scrambling into the bed of the truck. Tim said her name and looked at his mother and tried to smile, and then Lucas was in the truck giving him a hypodermic needle, calling to Livy to run to the house for blankets. Cordelia cried out when Lucas took the shirt off Tim's poor feet, but he handed her a roll of gauze and told her to help him and she did, wrapping the blackened stubs after he slathered them with salve.

Hallie climbed into the cab of the truck with whoever was

driving, and the rest of them—he, Lucas, Cordelia, and Livy—
rode in the back with Tim. Lucas hooked up a bag of plasma
while Livy covered Tim, first with a white sheet and then blankets. It's funny how the brain remembers certain details, like
the white sheet she draped gently over him, thinking it would
be better against his scorched skin than the woolen blanket. She
and Cordelia lay on either side of him, warming him with their
bodies. The morphine had eased him and he closed his eyes and
rested.

The hospital scenes return at odd times, always when Carl
is least expecting it, moving like an old celluloid movie he's got
locked in his head. Squiggly-patterned chairs in a white hallway, coffee machines, alien instruments beeping each time the
door to Tim's room opened or closed. Lucas's face was black
with soot; Carl had rinsed his face in the bathroom so the ash
and soot were on his clothes and shoes and the skin he wasn't
able to reach with the paper towels. He and Livy went into the
room several times and at one point Tim was sitting up and
seemed almost happy, no pain at all. Not wanting them to get
their hopes up, Lucas explained that the burns were so deep that
Tim's nerve endings had been destroyed and the euphoria was
the result of that. The sensory apparatus was dumping into his
bloodstream and would soon clog the kidneys. He died early the
next morning, all of them at his bedside.

Carl doesn't remember sitting down, but his back is against
a fir, and Cordelia is sitting beside him, her head on his arm,
weeping softly. He remembers the sound of weeping, not here
but at home in Minneapolis, where she stayed with them the rest
of that summer. Each night Hallie would slip out of their bed
and into Cordelia's. He'd see them in the morning when he left
for the office, their bodies curled like spoons in the bed. Hallie's

love was unquestioning and patient—she seemed to know instinctively how much or little Cordelia needed. That fall Cordelia returned to Berkeley to start teaching, but in December resigned and took a research position at the Missouri Botanical Garden. She'd been offered it earlier, she explained, but had turned it down because of the excessive travel, not wanting to be apart from Tim that long. "The job is still open," she said, "so I'm taking it. It's important work and, well, I think it's what I should be doing right now."

It is hard for him going back; several times they have to stop so he can rest. When they reach the other side of the meadow, where the path through the woods intersects with the summer road, Cordelia helps him to sit and hikes back to get the car. He is grateful to stretch out his legs on the sandy ground, grateful too when she returns, and they drive the rest of the way in silence. Every joint in his body aches. She hands him the water bottle and he drinks.

He is shaken, the air moving with black dots, when she helps him out of the car and across the yard to the new house, where Hallie is standing in the kitchen slicing tomatoes.

"You hungry?"

He doesn't answer. The fire is in his neck and legs, and his stomach roils at the thought of food. Instead of resting, which he knows he should do, he climbs laboriously up the narrow spiral stairs. He doesn't feast on the polished wood or the cleverness of the bookshelves he built into the side of the staircase. With each step he feels the painful reverberations in his ankles and calves. Titles weave and pitch, and he has to grip the railing hard and concentrate on remaining upright.

By the time he reaches the safety of the top floor and his chair, he has lost all feeling in his legs. He does not weep, for the disease has stolen his tears, but he is conscious of a weak, guttural gasp sputtering from his throat, a sob perhaps, not unlike the sound a frog makes. Soon he will be an exile in his own house. It is only a matter of months, the doctor said, before he will lose the use of his limbs. He will not be able to climb the stairs to the bedroom or study. Nor will he ascend to the roof and study the stars. He will be limited to the lower bedroom and the kitchen, the only levels accessible to a wheelchair.

How oblivious he'd been as he sat at the wooden table in the white cabin dreaming of their future house. Sat with his long, supple arms and legs, his strong back, his functioning sweat glands, his youth and happiness. He winces at the irony: this tall, tiered house with its spiral staircase suited for healthy legs and a fully functioning skeleton. Like the vegetable and wood-land gardens, his favorites, across the stone bridge, closed off by his own design.

He knots and unknots his hands, fidgets with paper on the surface of the desk, roots around for some object to throw. There, erasing the sunlight, is a familiar profile. Something passes be-tween them, an unconscious wave of energy that eases the ten-sion in his hands and legs.

"As the disease progresses, my brain will become a prisoner in a body that no longer functions. Here, I'll draw it for you." He pulls a sheet of paper toward him and opens his box of col-ored pencils. Slowly, willing his hand to obey, he draws a peacock-colored sponge with bulging eyes peering out from the prisonlike bars traversing the surface of the head, the body shrunken into a fetal position, a yellow-colored tube emerging from the tiny penis.

"I've always said that if I had to choose my most cherished organ, I'd choose the brain. Cancer might have been quicker, though, and I'd have kept my voice. That's the kicker—eventually I won't be able to talk. There I'll be, lucid as a new day, unable to talk or feed myself or have sex or go to the bathroom except in a tube."

He clenches his hands on the edge of the desk. "What do *you* know? To have everything you've ever wanted taken away from you. Not *thrown* away, I didn't say that. I've made mistakes. I've shut myself off, hurt people. But I wasn't the total idiot *you* were."

He smashes his pencil against the paper, breaking the point. Whips it back and forth across the surface of the desk until the tip of the pencil shreds the paper and scratches the wood beneath. He flings the pencil against the glass door, followed by the box of pencils, then the water bottle, and drops his head onto the desk. A noise next to him and he rears up. "Get out, *go!!*" he yells, but the specter is gone. Hallie stands at his shoulder.

"Carl?" she asks, shaken.

He stares at her, blinks, then turns his head away. "Leave me alone, Hal."

"Can I bring you something to eat?"

He laughs bitterly. "So I can stay strong and healthy? No thanks."

"Carl . . ."

"You'll be able to talk to me until you're blue in the face. I won't be able to argue back or shut you off or do anything other than listen."

Her blue eyes swim with tears and she walks purposefully away. A surge of self-hatred sweeps over him as he thinks about what a crank he is, how much uglier even than this he'll become, dependent and useless, worse than a child.

When he wakes, he is lying on the couch in his study and can tell by the light that it is late afternoon. He stretches his legs and watches the emerald frieze shimmer along the edges of the room. It is his favorite time of day—the woods still, sun low in the sky, windows revealing multiple layers of green and gold. He must have slept several hours. Emptiness weighs on him, as if his internal organs have been scooped out, leaving only the bony shell. His tongue feels cottony and he looks for the water bottle as he pulls himself slowly up. Remembering his tantrum earlier, he shuffles to the glass door and bends to pick it up. Empty, the water a pale stain on the rag rug. *You are your own worst enemy,* he thinks.

For the second time that day he is aware of his father's presence in the room and turns. Even a ghost might help to ease the emptiness he feels, the yawning gulf of his own death ahead. Tommy is leaning against the door, the image blurred but recognizable. It is so odd, he thinks, looking into the face of your father and he is twenty years younger than you. "What? Are you a symptom of the disease, or my buried past come to haunt me?" Passing the doorway, he waves his hand but it is only air, the warm feel of the wooden door frame. "You have no idea how terrible it is to find out that the person you've given your life to could fall in love with someone else."

A stirring in the empty space around him, as if a low electric current is passing through. "I used to think you deserved it, dying like that." He sighs. "But I don't anymore." He imagines those moments in the car, the only witness to Tommy's fiery death a woman he barely knew. No time to say good-bye or make amends. What would that be like, facing death with no one you love, and no one who loves you, by your side? "Mom loved you till the day she died. I thought it was a weakness in her, a lack of self-respect. Now I think *you* were the weak one. Her forgiving you . . ." He pauses. "I think it just showed her capacity to love. I get that."

He limps stiffly down the spiral staircase and into the quiet kitchen. The counter is clean and there is no sign of dinner. He fills a glass of water and drinks heartily, water spilling onto his neck and shirt. Hearing music from the summer cabin, he leaves the house and walks across the prairie, noting the newly mowed paths and grass. When he sees that Cordelia's car is gone, he plummets. He wishes he'd seen her off, thanked her, at least, for mowing. Hallie turns from the sink when he enters the kitchen and says, brightly, without any residue from their conversation earlier, "I've made a cold soup for dinner with berries from the berry farm. Cory and I went out while you were sleeping and picked them."

"When did she leave?"

"Half an hour ago."

"We're eating here, then?"

"Yes, do you mind?"

He shakes his head. "Can I help?"

She smiles gratefully. "It's all done. You could pour me a glass of wine."

Contrite over his bad humor earlier in the day, he pours each of them a glass of white wine, places hers on the counter, and walks onto the porch, easing himself into the Adirondack chair. The goldfinches scatter but he is patient, knowing it will take only a minute for them to return, which they do, sending the feeder spinning. The whirring hummingbirds hover above the spouts of the nectar-filled feeder at the far end of the porch.

His head bobs forward involuntarily and he focuses on holding it upright, wishing he'd brought the brace. *Hold her head up, like this,* the nurse told him. He took the infant into his arms, small head bobbing like a rag doll's, too heavy for the undeveloped muscles of the neck to lift. Aging, illness—the slide back to infancy—it's nauseating. At the touch of Hallie's hands on his shoulders, he jumps, knocking his wine glass onto the floor. She disappears into the kitchen for a towel to wipe up the spill and hands him a fresh glass.

"I'm sorry," he says. "You startled me."

She moves forward and places her hands again on his shoulders. "Your neck?"

He nods, unable to speak. Slowly she kneads the muscles in his shoulders and upper back, her hands tentative at first but gaining confidence and strength as she travels up his neck and into the base of his skull. He moans, rocketing between the gratified give of his muscles and the overwhelming pleasure he feels at the touch of her hands.

"Come over here and lie down," she says, guiding him up and out of the chair. Before he has time to think, they are across the room and he is lying on his stomach on the daybed. She climbs onto the bed and places her knees on either side of his hips, resting on her heels as she pulls his shirt up and over his head. Like they've done dozens of times before only not for a long time and not like this, his mind still wary but his heart and body opening, releasing under the pressure of her hands on his lower back, the light rocking of her body as she works her thumbs along his spine.

Suddenly her palms are filled with oil and she is massaging him in large, moving circles. He's a desert, the cells of his body drinking incessantly. It is surprising not only how good it feels but also how good she is at it. The back rub is not her strong suit, a fact that has always disappointed him, he loving to be touched and she too often reserved—*lazy*, he's thought at times, not willing to work hard enough to please him.

Now, however, she is completely engaged, following the map

of muscle and bone, the spongy flesh in his arms. He remembers her hands on his back that day on the beach at Torremolinos, their money almost gone and only a few days left of their honeymoon. Her skin from weeks of sun was burnished the copper of her hair—he lost his breath just looking at her. She reaches beneath him and unbuckles his belt, undoes the button on his trousers, his zipper, then slides his pants the length of his legs and onto the floor. He is awash in memory and desire, the pitch climbing as she works the oil into his buttocks, thighs, legs, wrings his shins the way he likes. When she pulls each toe taut and rubs oil between them, he trembles.

She stands a moment, hesitant, then swiftly removes her clothes, taking his outstretched hand as he rolls over and guides her on top of him. Running his fingers up her arms, he traces the rosy blush coloring her neck and chest. For a moment he stops, lets his hands still as she gazes down at him and he up at her—so many years between them, love and hurt and anger and joy and regret and change, the familiar blue of her eyes, the deep worry line in her forehead, her smell—then he circles her neck with his hand and pulls her toward him, covering her mouth with his, shuddering as her warm breasts reach him and she presses her pelvis to his.

He coats her in oil, visiting each part of her body, a landscape he knows intimately, touching her the way she likes, slowly and skillfully until she is on the cusp of coming and then he enters her, stunned by the intensity of his lust, even more by how well his body performs, weakened into near infancy only an hour ago and now as close as he's been in years to the ecstasy of their earlier lovemaking. After, they lie spent, spooned into each other like the old days, his arm wrapped across her right shoulder and breast and hand held tightly in hers, her leg coiled over his.

How long before his body will be incapable of lovemaking? He sighs, and in her fall into sleep she hears, or senses, and tightens her grip on his hand. All his life he has focused on the work, the next big project—places, buildings—perfect and made to last. Now, everything feels mortal and endangered. *Im*perfect. Thinking of the project, he can't help but smile at the irony in it: the blasted landscape and the structures he and his team are designing, built to be moved, taken apart, reconfigured and remade. When the research center is built, *if* it's built, he will be but fragments of bone and ash.

He wakes to flickering lights in the meadow. Expecting lightning, he looks up, but the sky is clear, moon shining and stars. Maybe his eyes are playing tricks on him, but there it is again: tiny blazes of silver light, muting into a milky memory of itself. Fireflies. More in the grasses, the air, the branches of trees.

Chapter 10

Caddis Wood (September)

Hallie studies him, distressed by the arduousness of the outing he has proposed.

"We'll take the wheelchair," he says. His face has that familiar, determined look: *Of course we can do this. What is your problem?*

"The paths are too narrow, honey. With the rain last night, there will be mud, downed branches . . ."

"We'll stay on the summer road. *Please*, Hallie."

She gnaws her lip, not wanting to refuse him. It is unfair perhaps, the latitude he demands from her because he is dying. She fills the water bottle and folds a light blanket into her backpack. He holds on to her arm as they push the wheelchair toward the blue van parked in the drive. Alex convinced her to lease rather than buy a van, helped her to choose the simplest, easiest vehicle to operate. After settling Carl in front, she slides into the driver's seat and backs carefully into the lane.

The road's green tunnel is riddled with gold—tall roadside grasses turned to maize, aspens raining quaking yellow leaves. The van crosses the first car bridge, passes Joe and Marnie Pratt's, and climbs the lane into the deeper woods. Colors simmer as the sun, breaking through, transforms the hardwoods into a panoply of red and gold. Hallie takes the fork in the summer road toward Osprey Meadow and drives until the road ends in a small clearing.

They walk the path about two hundred yards, Carl using the wheelchair as support, before he signals her to stop. It saddens her how heavily he leans on her as she guides him onto the seat of the wheelchair. She hands him the water bottle and waits for him to drink. The road is wet and rutted from last night's rain, and as she pushes the chair across leafy ground, she smells the moldering earth. Every few minutes she needs to bend down and work the wheels free of clotted leaves. Webs spun in morning sunlight break across her face. Carl points to mushrooms scalloping a downed birch like scales on a fish.

It's easy to track the course of the fire, and she can see it now without a well of grief obliterating the view. The blackened landscape and charred stumps have receded beneath a riot of ferns, shrubs, and saplings. Sadly, she marks the contrast between her husband's deteriorating body and nature's furious fecundity. Ten minutes later, the path terminates at the edge of a slight rise overlooking the vast, rippling bowl of grasses and sedge.

Carl is right, of course. Of all the places in the woods to view the flaming leaves, this is the best. Together they gaze across the rolling grass, moved by the multitude of tones, the rim of smoldering trees. She remembers other glorious Indian summer days they came here—sometimes with the girls, more often alone—the air warm and blessedly free of insects.

She removes the blanket from her pack, spreads it out, and guides him out of the wheelchair and onto the ground. Kneeling, she leans back on her ankles and pulls him, in a seated position, gently against her, supporting his head on her breast. The sun shimmers on the meadow. She reaches for the comb in the pocket of his sweater and runs it gently across his scalp and down the length of his white hair. He murmurs softly in pleasure. At times like these he doesn't let on if he is aware of her silent grief, the tears that well and spill over, sudden and unconscious. Occasionally she thinks, *It is good to have so much time to prepare.* At other times it doesn't seem to matter—there is no end to the sorrow she feels, the fear of what is to come. As difficult as it is witnessing the deterioration in his body, it is impossible to imagine what it will be like to wake up without him there.

After she finishes combing his hair, she braids her hands across his chest and rocks them slowly back and forth. He dozes, his breathing clear and regular. Tipping her head back, she drinks in the warm sun, wanting to hold the moment, the feel of his body in her arms, as long as possible. When they were younger, they made love in this place. She remembers the weight of his body, the sun, his face inches from hers.

A sudden whoosh in the air and she feels before she sees a flock of wild turkeys land not twenty yards in front of them, on the edge of the meadow. Their backs are to her, dun gray and brown feathers, long legs, white heads with yellow beaks. They cluck noisily as they amble into and through the long grass.

After he wakes, they sit awhile before starting back. The return is harder, as the road rises slightly and she has to push the wheelchair the entire way. Joe's pickup truck is parked in the drive when they pull in. Joe is a genius at showing up and working while they're occupied with something else. He and Dennis Malloy, a local carpenter, have removed the thresholds between rooms in the summer cabin, built a ramp to the back door, and made the bathroom accessible. He's also installed a small, highly efficient furnace and air-conditioning unit. An unequivocal fan of the new house next door, which he helped to build, Joe took some convincing to admit that the design—the small, efficient downstairs area, the bedrooms and study accessible only by means of a spiral staircase—would not work for an invalid. Nor did he seem to understand, having grown up in this landscape and so, perhaps, become immune to its beauty, Carl's desire to be as close as possible to nature. With the thresholds removed and the porch redone, Hallie will be able to wheel a hospital bed from room to room. Carl can spend his days and nights with only a screen between him and the woods and prairie.

Seeing Carl's drooping neck and pale complexion, Hallie wants to take him to the new house for a nap but he insists on viewing the work Joe and Dennis are doing on the porch. She wraps him tightly in the neck brace and wheels him into the light-filled room. It never ceases to surprise her how quickly he comes to life once he's in the midst of a new construction project. At the sight of the two men on ladders, floor thick with wood shavings, his color returns and he seems to rise several inches in the chair.

Hallie understands his victory at the sight of the large, floor-to-ceiling windows that hinge open like garage doors, giving the room and everyone in it the feeling of floating on grass. For years she nagged him to get rid of the windows, which he'd scavenged from a building site and moved from one storage shed to another, holding firmly to the conviction that he'd find a use for them. Now, the room can be used year-round, in every type of weather. The insulated glass and custom screens allow it to be as open or protected as they wish. Hallie leaves them to the work and walks next door to make lunch.

As she enters the kitchen she hears the telltale hum of the fax machine and recognizes the NIH letterhead on the sheets of paper lying in wait. A long list of chemicals: *Cygon, Sevin, Kelthane, benomyl, malathion, folpet, diazinon.* At the bottom is a brief note:

Dear Mrs. Fens:

Dr. Schlain asked that I forward you this information. We entered the data from all of our Shy-Drager patients and one link the computer came up with is the following list of chemicals. As you know, we are engaged in ongoing research as to the causes of the disease. We will continue to keep you updated, especially if we find anything that might be helpful to you and your husband. Very truly yours,

Dr. Jeffrey Peters

She carries the list to the computer and types in the names for a Google search. What comes up: chemicals used in pesticides, insect control for roses, pesticide poisoning. Heart skipping, she takes the printout and strides purposefully to the shed, glad that the men are preoccupied on the porch. Organizing the shed was one of the projects she took on at the end of the summer; she would have completed the job sooner had it not been for Carl's refusal to get rid of half the junk she found in there. "It's not disorder," he argued, "if I know where everything is and what it might be used for." He prided himself on his ability to recycle and reuse, didn't like her poking around in his things. Eventually, however, he yielded, realizing without her having to put it into words that soon he would no longer be capable of using anything he had stored in the shed.

She remembers exactly where the cans and containers of pesticide and herbicide are and goes directly to them, maneuvering her way around the shredder, lawn mower, the girls' old bicycles, the cradles Carl made soon after the twins were born. A few weeks ago she boxed the chemicals to take to the hazardous waste dump in Spooner, but he stopped her. She'd overruled him on so many things that she couldn't bear another argument, though this one seemed so simple: the lawn, flowers, shrubs once needing these chemicals were gone, which was the beauty of the native prairie, so why hang on to this stuff? *Because,* he said, we still grow vegetables and while I'm using organic soaps and netting and mulching the heck out of it to keep back the insects, we may need to take drastic measures now and then. So she returned them to the shelf.

Now, she takes the boxes and cans down one at a time and drops them into a basket. The faint chemical smell leaking from the spray spouts permeates the back of the shed. Holding the basket in two hands, she carries it outside and empties the contents onto the grass. She then checks the ingredients against the list of chemicals on the printout.

Turning toward the meadow, she blinks away the tall waving grasses and wildflowers and conjures up the sight of the pristine lawn and tiered flower beds. She sees him, tall and lean, dark hair aglow in the sun, pointing his spray can at the drowsy flowers, dousing leafy herbs and vegetables. He zigzags tirelessly back and forth across the lawn, spreading herbicide into the grass.

With a deep sigh, she tosses the cans back into the basket and puts it in the trunk of her car. Her face is hot with tears. She hears the murmur of the men's voices and returns to the house, where she Googles directions to the toxic waste disposal site in Spooner, then busies herself with the routine work of making lunch. She carries a tray filled with sandwiches, fruit, and a pitcher of iced tea next door.

"Come on, boys," she calls, setting the tray down on the table in the living room.

Later, after she's cleaned up and gotten Carl to lie down in the cool of the new house, she checks her e-mail again. Her editor has sent her a new blurb for the Demeter and Persephone book.

After weeks of editing back and forth, the book is ready for production. She's happy with the positive reviews from the poets who have read the book. Much as she's tried to bring a new angle of vision to the myth, to maximize her knowledge and talent as a poet, she did not anticipate such a response. It's an old story, after all, and a score of well-known writers have taken it on. She would have been happy simply to have it published and the reviews respectable.

When she's finished, she moves to the table by the window and opens her notebook. She is restive, wishing herself back in the summer cabin where she works best. It should only be another week, Joe has promised, before he and Dennis can clear out, taking their work table, sawhorses, and tools with them. Given how hard the men have worked, and how the light here spills into Carl's beautifully designed kitchen, she feels guilty for her fussiness about where she works.

She's deep into a new sequence of poems, a project that has taken her completely by surprise. While nature has always been a subject in her poetry, she doesn't consider herself a "nature poet." Yet here she is, immersed in the biology and symbolism of the hyperaccumulator plants. Why can't science figure out a way for the human body to do what the plants can: suck up disease-carrying cells, flood themselves with antioxidants for protection, store the bad cells in miracle pockets, and then reduce, degrade, or turn them into harmless vapor? Better yet, restore the sick to their former selves. After weeks of research and reading, she has filled one journal with drafts of poems.

It isn't just about *you*, she thinks—architects and planners, engineers and scientists—though your work is certainly impressive. The nonhuman world is making the bigger sacrifice. If nature has a voice, what does it sound like? She doesn't want to objectify nature, make it human or godlike. She simply wants to honor the value of these plants and trees, whose miraculous adaptive properties are being used by humans to repair the damage they—*we!*—have done to the natural world.

She doesn't hear Carl rouse from his nap or walk slowly down the spiral stairs until he's standing over her. Looking up, she sees the purple rim beneath his eyes, the hunched posture as if the simple task of holding up his neck is too much for him. She hands him the printout from the fax machine. "We got a list from the NIH." His eyes widen as he reads. "They're chemicals in common household pesticides. It's the link between all of the Shy-Drager patients in Dr. Schlain's study."

He sits down next to her. "Shit."

She lays her head on his arm. "God help us."

She listens to the soft whirring of the ceiling fan, the ticking clock, the buzz of Joe's electric saw on the porch across the meadow. It would be nice to smash something, but then, once the impulse has been met, what are they left with? Finally, she stands.

"I'm going to take the cans of pesticide into Spooner."

"Today?" His face is very pale.

"Yes. I don't want them in the house or the shed or anywhere else on the property."

"Want me to come?"

She shakes her head. "Do you need anything before I go?"

"No. I've got a conference call with Alex and others at the office. Hallie?"

She turns at the door.

"If only we *knew*." He holds out his hands and drops them in a gesture of defeat.

She smiles sadly at him and leaves. She can't stay in the house another minute, can't look at him, can't look at the meadow, the stream, the new windows on the porch, the vegetable or herb garden, the shed, the turning leaves, Joe or Dennis or their tools or truck or their earnest, sweaty faces. On the drive to Spooner she focuses on the long, narrow road unspooling ahead of her through banks of burnished trees. Rolling down the window, she breathes in the spicy smell of decaying leaves and chimney fires. The air is loud with the honk of migrating geese and rattle of abandoned corn shocks. By the time she arrives at the dump in Spooner and deposits her basket of cans and containers, she is calm, as if she is running a normal errand on an ordinary day.

On her drive back, she stops at the apple orchard and buys a bag of fresh-picked fruit. Nothing like a house filled with the fragrance of baking apples. When she passes the turnoff to the Howells' house, she pulls over without thinking, parks, and strides into the red pine grove. The ground is soft with needles, broken by clusters of browning lady fern, and in a few minutes she is inside the heart of the grove. The pines are planted in uniform rows, so it's like looking down an aisle of gray stems, skeins of sunlight flickering at the far end.

After standing a moment to acclimate herself, Hallie lies on the spongy ground and gazes up through woven shadows of light and dark. Wind gusts and the pines creak and moan as they move. Like old people's bones, she thinks, stiffened after a long sleep. As she listens, the creak gives way to sighing leaves and then the rush of waves. She follows the winking light in the spires, the shuddering swell as they rock back and forth. Sound washes over her, wave upon wave, its pine-scented breath on her face. Tears come fast and sudden and she weeps for a long time. Her sobs mingle with the rustling leaves and wind.

That night she wakes abruptly from a dream: snow falling at the end of the alley, only it's no longer an alley but the hill near their home in Minneapolis and the snow is falling on the windshield of a white station wagon speeding down a hill toward a tiny girl in a red hat. The red hat becomes a blue hat and there are two of them standing in the path of the car. She shakes her head to rid herself of the blood-spattered snow and tiptoes downstairs. Hot milk and brandy and several chapters of *The Portrait of a Lady* usually do it, but an hour later she is still awake. Flashlight in hand, she heads across the yard and around the summer cabin to the shed. She lifts one of the cradles—the two are stacked one inside the other—and carries it into the cabin and onto the half-finished porch. Settling into the Adirondack chair, she removes the pedal from inside the cradle and slides it onto the small bar Carl made to connect the two so they could be rocked together or one at a time. She touches her foot to the pedal and the lone cradle moves.

Moonlight turns the sky into a milky sea that billows into ribbons of red. Red and white and red and white. There in the chalky waves are the speeding car and Bea's red hat against the snow. She blinks and sees the mound of snow on the north end of the island. The girls had been outside all morning building an igloo out of the pile left by the snowplow. Hallie stepped outside the front door to call Bea inside for lunch and saw the white station wagon hurtling down the hill. She gasped and bolted down the steps. Snow clung to her calves as she ran, sluggishly, as if she was slogging through water. She shouted Bea's name, her eyes on the mound of snow under the crab apples, the speeding, spinning vehicle.

The red pom-pom on Bea's hat bobbed into sight, her head cocked as if she was listening. The car, having spun completely around on the ice, was careening straight toward the heap of snow where Bea was working on her igloo. Hallie screamed "STOP!"

and then "RUN, BEA!" waving her arms over her head, thrusting her body through the snow. Hearing her mother, Bea turned away from the fort, was standing up facing Hallie when the station wagon crashed through the crab apples. "BEA!" Hallie screamed, reaching her arms toward her daughter. Bea turned just as the car hit the wall of snow and rose up over it like an enormous arctic beast. The front corner of the car caught her on the side of the head, hurling her through the air.

She landed a few feet from Hallie and sank noiselessly into the snow. Hallie fell to her knees and brushed the flakes from Bea's face, afraid to touch or move her. She had heard the screaming even as Bea was hit, not sure if it was her voice or someone else's. Bright-red blood pooled in the collar of Bea's snowsuit. Hallie recognized Cordelia's voice, that it had been *her* scream she'd heard, as the girl reached her side. She was shivering, her voice ragged, eyes jumping from Hallie to Bea.

The screen buzzes so loudly that Hallie jumps, realizing the flashlight lying on the floor is still on and has attracted several night moths. For a moment she watches the useless, beating wings, marveling at the insects' ignorance and tenacity, unable to figure out a way in or a way out—until she turns the light off and the struggle ceases. *There is no stopping it,* she tells herself. No bringing him back the way they brought back Bea. No matter what she or the doctors or their daughters or Jack or Lucas or anyone does, he is going to die and she will go on living. She will wake up every morning and he will be gone.

CARL

Chapter 11

Caddis Wood (November)

He feels her kiss on his forehead and rouses. After pushing the wheelchair onto the porch, she adjusts the neck brace. Much as he dislikes the awful thing, he dreads even more being confined to the hospital bed. Cordelia, Beatrice, and Jack will arrive soon and he does not want them to see him carted around like a vegetable.

"I wouldn't exactly say a vegetable," Hallie says dryly.

"You try spending your day like this. Give me one more Thanksgiving upright as a man."

She positions the chair close to the large, hinged window. Despite the cold, she opens the window a few inches so he can hear the stream.

In addition to all the preparations for the holiday, she has to help him manage the pain in his neck and increased weakness and fatigue. She's been getting ready for days—baking, tidying the houses, making up the beds. Plus, it's been snowing off and on all week, and she's had shoveling to do. Today she rose early to make the stuffing for the turkey. He hears the squeak of the ironing board, her feet crossing the living room as she puts on a new CD. Ironing soothes her. He's never figured out why, probably the mindlessness of it, but it works. She'll iron her mother's

Irish linen tablecloths and napkins and set the table. She treasures the things Maeve continues to send: books, the Irish linens, Waterford crystal glasses.

He gazes up at the sky, the color of sheet iron, heavy with impending snow.

"It's going to snow again," she says, as if reading his thoughts.

"Yes."

"You think the roads are all right?"

"I'm sure they're fine."

Cordelia drove to Minneapolis yesterday, staying overnight at the house so she could pick up Beatrice and Jack at the airport. At noon she phoned, saying that Beatrice and Jack arrived on time from Seattle and they were on their way. It's almost two, so with slower going on the roads they should be here by two thirty. It will be a shock for Bea to see him, his legs and arms almost useless, his speech halted and slurred.

He pushes his mind toward the silver aspens on the hillside. Trunks, matted leaves, hard earth all dun and metal except for two green spruces in front of the cabin, red and white pines to the west. His view up the stream is unencumbered by leaves, and he can see the slate-covered water as it curls round the edge of the property and disappears into the swamp forest below the shed.

When he closes his eyes now, he hears their voices, like a movie playing alongside the present: two reels running simultaneously. Sometimes the images appear side by side, or they leapfrog over each other; at other times they're transposed like a double exposure. Now he sees Cordelia plowing steadily through the snow, her snowshoes leaving even tracks as she pressed forward. She was out ahead, as usual, Jack about ten yards behind, followed by Hallie, then Bea, Carl in the rear. He must have had

Shy-Drager's even then, for at fifty-eight he'd had no trouble keeping up with Cory. That day, though, he'd gotten winded early, had felt the strain in his back and legs. It was the winter before the illness started; the girls and Jack had come the weekend before New Year's, and the five of them had gone snowshoeing. He wonders if this Thanksgiving will be the last time the family is gathered in a festive way, when he can partake of their merriment.

Carl passes his hand in front of his eyes as a deer appears on the ridge and loops deftly in and out of the tree trunks, followed by another deer, and another, eight altogether, a herd gathering speed as they bound down the hill. Water eddies around their hooves. They stop, peer cautiously, dip their long necks into a bed of still-blooming watercress. If he calls out to Hallie, they will scatter. The deer are skittish with fear. It is deer-hunting season, and the woods, even their fourteen hundred acres supposedly off-limits except to members, are riddled with orange men. Hallie continues to worry that someone will be shot: "If one of the girls or Jack gets hurt, I'll do something horrible. I swear it."

And yet, he thinks, *try as we might, we cannot always protect them.* When he thinks of his daughters, sadness wells up within him. He is haunted by thoughts of their future, all that will go on without him. He worries that he'll be forced to look on, unable to intervene when he sees, as the dead might, what is coming. It's what purgatory is, he believes, being forced to observe your loved ones' inevitable suffering, as well as the pain caused by your own failures and inadequacies. There's no going back, of course. Just as now there's so little opportunity to go forward, to say or write down all the things he wants to say.

Resting his head against the chair, he listens to the steady, rippling stream. The remaining leaves on the red oak rustle with a high-pitched singing sound. How stubborn they are, holding their leaves long after the other hardwoods have shed. Did his father have to watch the sorrow and pain he'd caused his wife and son, look on helplessly as Nan raised Carl and then died alone in a hallway, no one to help her? *Is that why you're here? Is this your purgatory, then, to roam a shade on the earth until I die?* A flash of white tail feathers and he identifies the northern junco's loose trill, the tickering notes as it flies away.

He hears laughter, and Cordelia and Tim splash past the bridge, heading upstream. It was high summer: ferns fringed in gold, yarrow turned chocolate, first leaves gone pale ocher. Cory and Tim were hunting frogs, studying them for deformities, taking samples of stream and pond water and sediment. It was good to hear the two of them laughing. Their research had made them angry and grim, and their usual spirited conversations at dinner were replaced by a litany of woe: frogs with twisted spines, malformed hind legs, missing and contorted legs and digits, webbed skin. The chemical compounds in the water, Tim said, were products of various pesticides, herbicides, and fertilizers used by farmers in the area. All of it pouring into the watershed. *And me*, he thinks, *as malformed now as one of Tim's frogs.*

What would Tim think of the latest report from Katie Moran and her colleagues at the Minnesota DNR? Animal populations dropping, animals migrating north, algae blooming in the pond, stream levels sinking, their beloved feather mosses and lady's slippers becoming scarce.

Carl hears the muted hum of a car engine, slamming doors, and Hallie's welcoming cry from the yard. A duffel bag appears and then Jack in a gray parka, trim black beard and hair. "Hey!" he calls, involuntary alarm on his face at the first sight of Carl giving way to an infectious smile. A flash of gold as Beatrice enters, blue eyes and outstretched arms rushing toward him. She is on her knees, burying her face in his neck. He tries to raise his hand, wanting to touch the tumble of strawberry waves, but he can't. He feels the tension in her body, knows she is hiding her face from him.

Cordelia and Hallie crowd the far end of the kitchen. Cordelia is in tune with the alterations in his body, knows what he's still capable of—how active and facile his mind remains—so watches, brow furrowed, impatient with her sister for making such a spectacle. *It's all right,* he wants to say. *She's not here every week like you—it's a shock for her.* Jack moves forward and gently untwines Bea's arms from Carl's neck. As she pulls back, she swipes at the tears on her face and smiles at him.

"I had to wear one of these once," Jack says, pointing to the brace. "Got a nasty whiplash. We were seventeen and had just consumed half a bottle of whiskey in my dad's car. God, was he furious." He pulls Bea out of the way as Cory unceremoniously pushes past her to guide the wheelchair into the living room. There is much chatter as they undo and hang up hats and coats. Jack takes his and Bea's bags to the house next door. Huge, falling flakes catch on Jack's hair and parka as he walks through the pines.

Turning slightly, all his poor neck can manage now, even with the brace, Carl sees the girls framed in front of the milky mirror atop the bureau in their old room, which Hallie, with Livy's help, painted yellow with a garland of tiny pink and purple flowers. Cordelia is whispering to Bea. Telling her how to behave, he thinks. He wishes she would let it alone, give Beatrice the chance to find her own way, not try to manage everything. Even Hallie has struggled recently with Cordelia's ferocious determination to keep him alive as long as possible. He doesn't want the weekend to devolve into a battle over who knows best how to care for him.

Hallie carries a tray of snacks past him and places it on the low table between the couches. The girls call her into the bedroom and her face joins theirs in the mirror. Bea chides Hallie for being so thin. She *is* thin, he realizes, her loss of weight so slow and gradual he's hardly marked it. He's grown so dependent on her, needs her for so many humble daily tasks, that he's amazed at her tirelessness and strength. As he studies her now, however, standing alongside their daughters, he sees the shadows on her face, the way the sweater hangs from her shoulders.

Their voices change pitch as they talk, take on a playful, almost childlike tone—a special language and cadence reserved only for each other. He assigns it the place he has for other instinctive looks and behaviors—the fondness and occasional forbearance they offer *him*. Even as children, the girls showed him a protectiveness they didn't offer to Hallie. As if they couldn't bear to hurt his feelings or see him disappointed. To have you disappointed in *them*, Hallie has told him. Their confidences, their news and hard questions have always been reserved for Hallie. Also their anger and impatience. She's resilient, they seem to say; she can take it. They count on her goodness to them, her unconditional love.

When Jack returns, he brings in the wine and glasses and they drink a toast to the day and to each other. Though it is only three thirty, the afternoon is darkening and Hallie has turned on the lamps. Fire crackles in the stove. Carl drinks in the girls' faces, how alike and yet different they are as they stand side by side. Cordelia is lean and willowy like her mother, her shiny black hair cut short since she moved to St. Louis and went to work in the field; Beatrice is all peaches and cream to Cory's rich olive, a sprinkling of freckles, with Hallie's glistening russet hair. And then there's Hallie, the familiar worry on her face turned to happiness now that the girls have arrived.

While Hallie and the girls busy themselves in the kitchen, Jack pulls a chair next to him and they talk. He expects this from Jack, anticipates it with eagerness. Jack asks him about the office, the river research center, the landscape remediation.

"How do you keep up with everything? Do you and Hallie drive to the Cities regularly?"

Carl smiles. "Not so much anymore. I'll show you tomorrow morning—I have my office next door set up for teleconferencing."

He asks about the HMO where Jack works, his patients, the sailboat. They talk about Bea—her health, her job teaching music in a private high school. Jack quizzes him about the medications he's taking, the disintegration of his body as the disease becomes more advanced. Carl appreciates his frankness when he asks what to expect and how they will handle it.

The table with its extra leaves takes up the large area in front of the stove. Hallie pats down a corner of the crisp white linen as she sets a bowl of mashed potatoes on the table. Cory wheels Carl to the head of the table as Hallie, Bea, and Jack carry in more dishes: broccoli and almonds, homemade cranberry sauce, liver and oyster stuffing, squash, steaming gravy. Cory fills everyone's glass with wine. Finally, they are all seated. They look expectantly toward Carl, who bows his head as Cory on one side and Bea on the other take his hands in theirs, and he gives thanks that they are all here, together. Others chime in, adding to the list of blessings. They raise Maeve's Waterford crystal glasses, Cory holding up hers and Carl's, and toast. Talk erupts and the food is passed. The girls heap spoonfuls onto his plate; he knows he won't be able to finish it all, but he lets them do it anyway. Bea watches transfixed as Cordelia deftly cuts his meat and lifts the fork to his mouth.

After they've been eating awhile, Jack clears his throat, taking Bea's hand in his. "We have news."

"Oh, Jack, let's wait until later," she says.

"Wait for what?" Hallie asks.

"Come on, honey," Jack says. "Tell them."

Cory wipes Carl's mouth with his napkin and puts the spoon down on the plate, waiting expectantly. Jack is beaming.

"Okay, well," Bea looks round the table and smiles. "We're having a baby."

Hallie cries out and runs over to Bea, throwing her arms around her. Carl swallows, feeling the lump in his throat, his happiness for Bea and Jack, the wonderful thought of a baby, vying with a needle of anxiety.

"What does your neurologist say?" Cory asks.

Immediately a pall falls over the room. "About what?" Jack asks.

"About the risks for you in having a baby." She looks around the table—at him, at Hallie, seeking reinforcements. Hallie shakes her head, as if to signal, *Wherever you're going with this, stop.*

"Bea, I want you to have a baby—I *do*. But it might be dangerous for you. You know this."

Bea's eyes turn flinty as she gazes at her sister. "Do you think I'd go ahead with this, or that Jack would agree to it, if there were a threat to my or the baby's well-being?"

"Yes," Cory says, her eyes flashing, "I do, if you wanted it badly enough. The doctors advised you not to have a baby." She takes a deep breath. "You could have adopted."

"Bea is in excellent health," Jack says. "Her neurological tests . . ."

Bea puts her hand on his arm. "Whatever's going on with you, Cory, you need to stop. My doctors gave us the green light to have a baby. I'm going to be *fine*."

Cory stands up, dropping her napkin on the table. "You're taking a huge risk. You know it." She looks round at the group. "You *all* know it—don't act like you don't."

Hallie stands. She doesn't make a move, however, knowing well enough not to reach out or interfere. They watch in silence as Cordelia puts on her coat and leaves the house.

"She's been in a bad mood ever since she picked us up," Bea says. "Pissed with our luggage taking so long, pissed at the snow . . ."

"She doesn't want me to die," Carl says. He looks around at them, wishing death out of the room so things don't have to be this heavy, so he doesn't need to see the spooked look on their faces. "It's only natural given what she's lived through. Now she's worried that something's going to happen to you." He reaches across the table toward Bea, who gets up and walks over to him. He cannot lift his arms to hug her so he rubs his face against the side of hers when she lowers herself to kiss him.

"The due date's June fourteenth," Jack says.

The talk turns to the baby. They chatter about baby things, the contractor they've hired to turn the spare room into a nursery, the park across the street, whether or not to take a baby on a sailboat, take a pregnant Bea on a sailboat, which doula to choose.

"What's a doula?" Carl asks.

Hallie laughs. "A woman trained to help you through labor."

"It doesn't have to be a woman," Jack says, "though they usually are."

"You should have the baby in a hospital, Bea, with an ob-gyn," says Carl, worry flooding over him. "If there are any complications . . ."

"Dad, the doula doesn't deliver the baby—she works with us ahead of time and comes to the hospital when I'm in labor, acts as an advocate and source of support so I have the kind of birth I want. You've all got to stop *worrying.*"

He glances out the window, picturing Cory with her head bent, plowing through the snow. He's grateful the temperature's remained above freezing. Bea, Jack, and Hallie chatter on, their happy voices floating cloudlike around him. Although he wishes Cory would be more circumspect with her fears about the pregnancy, he understands them. The remarkable progress Bea's made since the accident doesn't erase the long-term effects on her brain and body of such a traumatic injury. He sighs, knowing he will never see this child, perhaps not know how it turns out for Bea, if she'll carry the baby to term, how she'll do after. He's grateful for his lack of tears, even though his eyes smart and burn. He doesn't want to mar the tone, to interfere with their happiness.

As Jack and Bea busy themselves with clearing the table, Hallie comes round to him and wheels him into the bathroom, knowing, as she always does, his needs. She helps him onto the toilet seat and stands alongside him, her hand resting on his shoulder. He is struggling with sudden, overwhelming fatigue. When he's done and back in the wheelchair, she kneels down and washes his face with a cold washcloth. "You look warm," she says quietly. He sighs deeply, touching his forehead to hers. "She'll be fine, honey," she says and kisses him lightly on the lips, then wheels him back into the living room.

Bea and Jack are doing dishes: Bea washing, Jack drying.

Hallie settles him beside one of the couches, across from the window where the outside light from the house illuminates the falling snow. She takes the tablecloth and shakes it out the back door.

"It's still snowing!" she calls, stamping her feet on the mat.

When the dishes are done, Bea walks to the window. "Should I go after her?"

"No," Hallie says. "Leave her be." After putting the tablecloth in the laundry basket, she heads to the wooden box on the bookshelf. "Let's play cards." She plucks several decks from the box and tosses one to Jack. "Check to see if it's a full deck."

"Spades or euchre?" Bea asks, sitting at the table next to Jack.

"Euchre," Carl says as Hallie wheels him over to the table.

They are four games in by the time Cory returns. She slaps her boots in the doorway and hangs up her coat. "I'm sorry," she says. In the silence, he hears the crackling logs. "Can I play?"

Jack slides his chair back and makes a place between him and Bea.

"We'll start a new set," Bea says, dealing her sister into the game.

He sleeps late the next morning, wakes alone in the bed. He's used to it now, knowing how much Hallie loves this early time of day. He drinks in the smell of coffee and baking carrot bread. The bedsprings in the girls' room squeak and groan as Cordelia bounds out of bed and pads quickly into the bathroom. After she joins her mother in the kitchen, he times his breathing to the rise and fall of their voices. Sometimes in the past he's felt shut out by the closeness between the girls and Hallie, his maleness setting him apart, making him feel like an interloper. Mostly, though, it has been a comfort to him; he is proud of the world he has helped to create for all of them. He knows how many times he let them down, the events he missed as the girls were growing up. If they feel any bitterness toward him, they do not show it. He is grateful for this unforeseen opportunity to work on a project with Cordelia, to have her close after so many years living away.

He calls out for Hallie and she comes, Cordelia right behind, to assist him into his chair. Cordelia leaves while Hallie helps him into a clean pair of underwear. It's only a matter of weeks until he won't be able to sit by himself. There'll be no room for modesty then, no way to shield his nakedness from anyone—daughter, nurse, friend—who comes to help.

Cordelia rejoins them and kneels next to her mother as they pass the lotion back and forth, massaging it into his flaking skin. He closes his eyes in pleasure as Cordelia kneads his shoulders and Hallie rubs lotion onto and around each finger. When they're finished, Cordelia lifts him while Hallie slides on his corduroy slacks, puts on a freshly ironed shirt and his favorite cardigan sweater. Hallie ties his shoes while Cordelia rubs apricot oil into his scalp. Gently she combs his unruly white hair, taking care not to scrape the dry skin on top of his head.

"Ready?" he asks, smiling at them.

"Ready," Cordelia answers, grinning with pride at his appearance.

The day hurtles forward. He wants to slow things down, desires more from each passing moment. Bea's happy shouts as she and Jack shovel the paths between the house and cabin, throw snowballs at each other that splat against the sides of the house. Cory's flushed face spilling through the door—face, legs, hands covered with snow. Scrambled eggs, sausage, plates piled high with letter pancakes, everyone laughing, talking over one another, Hallie bustling back and forth—more syrup, more coffee, more orange juice. Bea feeding him this time, focusing hard on how much to put on the fork, how fast to do it, not wanting to make a mistake. As if there *is* one, he thinks, grateful for her kindness.

After breakfast, Jack wheels him over the freshly shoveled path and into the sunny kitchen of the house. He directs Jack to the desk, where Carl picks up a slender black remote control device the size of a PalmPilot. Jack stops the chair a few feet from a rectangular screen on the wall.

"Ready," Carl says. There's the sound of a bell and the screen lights up.

"Ah," Jack says. "It's voice-activated. Wonderful."

"Office," Carl says next. A series of clicks and buzzes, and Alex Thorne's face appears on the screen. He waves, backs up, and another man and two women appear. In the room are a conference table with architectural drawings and several open laptops, a second large screen on the wall behind them. A plan of the research center appears on the wall screen, and they talk back and forth. Jack pulls up a chair and listens as they debate different elements of the design. Carl challenges two of the younger architects, and words fly swiftly back and forth. He's not happy with what they've done with several of the interior spaces, presses them for a different approach. They reason with him; he reasons back. They listen, nod, and set a time to talk again tomorrow.

The plans on the screen shift to the landscape, and he and Alex talk about the floating pods and walkways, the mesh systems that cover strategic parts of the dump. When they're finished and the screen goes dark, Carl shows Jack the drawings, explains the overall scope of the project.

"Who's paying for all of this?"

"The state is contributing the lion's share, there's some federal money available, and there's an aggressive fund-raising campaign, targeting the companies we know did substantial dumping, though they have no legal obligation to pay."

"Why not?"

"There are too many polluters—companies, individuals, organizations. State agencies themselves allowed hundreds of thousands of cubic yards of sludge ash to be deposited there in the late seventies and early eighties. It would cost the state a fortune to pursue all of the responsible parties and take appropriate legal action. Just about every small business and large industry in the east metro area dumped there, so it's easy asking for money. The big companies are all ponying up with contributions."

"And these magic plants I've been hearing so much about?"

"Hyperaccumulators. Hallie's writing poems about them." Carl stretches his body in the chair, tired from the exertion.

"Ready to go back?"

"Yes."

Midway across the walk, they hear the melodic notes of the keyboard. As they enter, Bea looks up and smiles, not missing a beat. The crisp sound of the keyboard has set the room humming. Hallie and Cordelia are seated at the table, photo albums spread out in front of them. Jack pushes Carl to the table alongside Cory, then walks to the couch nearest Bea, where he settles comfortably with a book.

Carl rests his head against the chair and drinks in Beatrice's alabaster skin and glowing hair. So like Hallie when he first met her, though she's quieter, more self-contained than her mother, more like him in temperament, whereas Cordelia has Hallie's fiery personality. He marvels at the intensity in Bea's face and body as she plays, drawn like a moth to its light. The way Jack was, he's told them, when he passed the children's ward in the hospital and saw her for the first time at the piano. Her face is like the surface of a pond—wind, sun, rain passing over it.

Beside him, Cory and Hallie turn the pages of the photo album, talking softly, crying out when they revisit a memorable moment from the past. "Oh, come, Bea, look!" Hallie exclaims, and Bea joins her mother and sister at the table. They are looking at pictures of themselves swinging from the rope over the swimming hole. Another of the two of them in their Fourth of July dresses racing through the dusky meadow. When they turn the page, it is the summer after Bea's accident. The girls are sitting on the steps of the playhouse and the difference between them is palpable. He remembers taking the picture: Cory waving an American flag, making bug eyes at the camera, Bea sitting in a hunched position, left shoulder inches higher than the right, one side of her face gazing at the camera, the other side frozen as if asleep.

"Do you remember it?" Cory asks.

"Not the accident. I remember not being able to talk right and the kids making fun of me because the two halves of my face were different and having to do fourth grade all over again. Some of my friends stayed friends but the others didn't. Remember Lucy Keil's sleepover—how she invited you and not me?"

"But Lucy was *your* friend," Cory says. "I didn't even like her. Mom must have made you stay home."

"I wasn't invited, Cor—*you* were. And you went."

"I didn't."

"Yes, you did. You went to other parties, too."

"I did?"

Bea nods. "And you wouldn't wait for me when we were walking fast and I couldn't keep up and you got so mad when I had my laughing attacks."

He's anxious, not wanting this tension between them. He looks at Hallie for direction, but she's busy straightening the little black corners on the photos.

"Jeez, I forgot all about those laughing spells," Cory says. "You were such a freak, Bea—no wonder nobody wanted to invite you anyplace."

"*You* were a little shit."

Cory nods. "I was."

"Remember when I brought you the keyboard?" Carl asks Bea.

The summer after the accident he bought the keyboard and brought it to Wisconsin. Hallie and the twins were spending weeks at a time at the cabin and he wanted Bea to be able to play, music being the only aptitude that was unaffected by her injuries. One evening, after playing a tape of Chopin's Étude in E Major, he listened dumbfounded as Bea played it note perfect on the keyboard. He walked into the living room, where she was sitting at the keyboard, wondering if by some coincidence Hallie had bought the sheet music for it, but there was nothing there, only Bea gazing placidly out the window.

"How did you do that?" he asked.

She shrugged. "I thought it was so beautiful and heard it in my head so I just sat down and played it."

"That keyboard saved my life," says Bea.

There was no way of knowing if Bea had always had this gift of playing by ear or if the damage to her brain had somehow created it. While it took two years for her to regain her physical and cognitive functions, her musical ability surged ahead. She took up the flute as well as the piano, and in college did a double major in music and music therapy for children. Of course, his mother had an extraordinary aptitude for music as well, and he often felt the same comfort listening to Bea that he'd felt as a boy doing his homework to the sound of his mother's piano through the wall.

Cory picks up her wedding album, and Bea and Hallie lean toward her as she turns the pages. Looking down at the photos, he remembers how hot it was that week and how worried they were that people would be too uncomfortable outdoors. Tim waves at the camera, handsome and happy in his linen suit. His optimism was indefatigable. "The weather will be perfect," he kept saying. "I *know* it."

He was right, of course. A few days before the wedding, a summer storm drenched the woods and blew away the heat and humidity. Images whirl like smoke in Carl's head: the white tent, blazing wildflowers, paths mown through the meadow, Cordelia walking alongside him, her hand on his arm, Tim standing in the clearing, photos on the ridge overlooking Echo Pond, dancing and eating and kissing and laughter, glowing lanterns, a full moon, and then Tim and Cordelia strolling down the lane with their pup tent and sleeping bags, everyone waving and shouting congratulations, the throb of the lantern through the pines.

Cordelia is weeping softly and Bea has wrapped her arm around her. Jack has gone into the kitchen and, from the smell of it, is making soup. Cordelia wipes her face, smiles, and squeezes her sister's hand. The three women rise and bustle into the kitchen to make sandwiches.

"Turkey, Dad?" Cory asks.

His eyes blur suddenly, as if covered with a veil of tears, though he knows that's impossible. "Yes, with all the trimmings—stuffing, lettuce, mayo. And a big, cold glass of Heineken."

"Hear, hear," Jack calls, carrying an armful of plates to the table. "And after lunch I'll break out my Cuban cigars."

"Outside with those," Hallie says to him.

"I'll join you," says Cory.

"Me, too," Carl says. "We'll drink beer and smoke cigars and whiz under the trees."

Everyone looks at him, mouths open. "Okay, no whizzing. I'd have to whiz in a bottle, anyway."

"Can we eat, please?" Hallie asks, pushing him to the table.

Carl moves his hand to rub her butt but it flops uselessly to his side. She slaps him gently, sensing the motion, bringing a pleased grin to his face.

He wakes in the dead of night, listens through the window, open an inch, for the sound that roused him. Hallie sleeps soundly beside him. He waits for his eyes to grow accustomed to the dark. The bedroom door is ajar a few inches, and he hears the outer door closing, the sound of logs, squeak of the stove door. Muffled voices—Cory's and Bea's. In the past, before they installed the furnace, the stove was the sole source of heat in the living room. He'd put electric heaters in the bedrooms, but sometimes the girls preferred to camp out in the living room near the stove. He would keep the stove going, getting up several times during the night. As the girls grew older, they fed the stove themselves.

He hears the poker, sparking logs, the stove door again. It's easy to imagine them huddled on the flokati rug, wrapped in the fleecy throws from the couches. He can make out bits and snatches of their conversation, not enough to know what they are talking about, which is good—he doesn't want to eavesdrop—just enough to savor the sound of their voices. He burrows into the covers, lulled by the overlapping layers of time: his adult daughters in the present, teenagers plotting late-night joy rides with Tim in Lucas's car, little girls reading aloud the gruesome tales from *The Yellow Fairy Book*.

CARL

Chapter 12

Caddis Wood (February)

He can hardly speak now, only manages to scribble a few words. Hallie is good at interpreting his broken sentences and sprawled lines. He is a book, its pages laid out in front of her, written in a language only she can understand. She resists the gradual wasting away of his body, insisting on his daily exercises, pouring lotion on his peeling skin, feeding him as if he is a growing child and not a dying man.

Each morning she rolls the hospital bed onto the porch and as close to the window as possible, raising it so he's in a sitting position and can see out. She cracks the window open a few inches. The drama in his head is as vivid as anything he sees on the television or DVD player. Sounds enter the constantly evolving film in his imagination: part real, part memory, part what happens when the different tracks collide and merge. He doesn't know how much is caused by the illness, the cells in his brain ossifying like the rest of his body. After years of intense industry, his mind and body filling and using each moment, he has become friends with slowness. He is acutely aware of his surroundings, of each tiny change in his body and in the world he can see and hear.

He hears the *pop, pop, bang* of frozen trees. Swelling fibers of wood bursting and cracking. The rustle of cattails beside the stream, the ruffed grouse striking the white pine's brittle branches, Hallie making coffee in the kitchen. He can hear his mother and father talking softly, thinking he's asleep—one of their happier moments, making plans for Sunday at the beach. He's in and out of the arcing waves, waits eagerly for the white froth to rise over his shoulder before he dives forward, bodysurfing the wave in to shore. Gritty sand against his stomach.

Soft clacking and crunching beneath the pines, snapping brush, skitters across frozen snow. Loud echo of a snapping branch, which clatters to the ground. Bittersweet berries flash orange on the bank and Bea in her red hat and Cory in her blue are rolling a head for the snowman. Tim's curly hair is uncovered. They wind Lucas's woolen scarf around the snowman's neck, put one of Carl's fishing hats on the head. Cory throws a snowball and they tumble over each other in the snow.

Sometimes he hears Alice's voice, which is impossible since she was dead by the time they bought the summer cabin. But he knows it's her. She and Hallie were right about the garden. All his grand schemes—flowers and shrubs and soil carted in, fertilizer, herbicide, pesticide, fences, screens. Nature laughing at him. Now, when spring comes, the meadow will bloom with native prairie grasses and wildflowers. Shrubbery planted along the edge of the house and meadow will provide food and cover for grouse, birds, the red fox family, woodchucks, and other animals. Hallie, with Joe's help, has kept up the vegetable garden, though he suspects she'll let it go once he's gone.

He hears other voices, too. They began as a whisper, more than the sounds and music nature made. He listened hard, thought his mind was playing tricks or that the disease had entered his brain and was causing auditory synapses to misfire. The whisper grew and multiplied, became a chorus, until one day the sounds held meaning for him. *Anima antiqua,* Alice wrote in her note-book, the spirit that's lived in a place for a long time. He hears it beneath the snow, the frozen ground. He hears it in the creak-ing branches, inside the whispering stream.

we are out we are inside the house   we were here before   we have our own lives hidden in the dark   we nest inside the walls, beneath the floor   we shudder and pop   tap tap tap   we're hungry   we sleep   we dig our roots deep we die   we return we listen we love in our own way   we remember   we are born in the dark we reach up toward the light

His mind is a camera, memories as sharp as photographs. The house on that first visit: dull brown linoleum, dusty books, gray husks on sills. In the closet hung Henry's parkas, flannel shirts, Alice's hand-knit sweaters. Beneath them boots, bathi-nette, Swedish linens. Photographs: Alice's mother against the Baltic Sea, Alice at age twelve—white middy blouse and knick-ers. Henry in his waders, Will in his marine's uniform. Hallie peers through the cloudy kitchen window. When she removes her hat, her hair tumbles like a rain of sugar maple leaves. He blinks and they are inside the tent and she is tweezing ticks off his body. In the light of the kerosene lantern against the walls of the tent, she takes off her blouse. He gazes at her graceful neck, the swing of her hair, her perfect breasts.

Hallie steps up behind him and wraps her arms around him, careful not to hurt him. For a moment he's unsure where he is, whether they are here on this porch on a winter morning or there, inside the tent, the house silent in the dark. The bird feeder spins and he remembers.

When he was a young man, he thought the body was every-thing. He looked at women, even after he was married, and lusted after their bodies. At night he'd wake and roll toward Hallie and just the feel of her skin or the smell of her hair made him harden with desire. He'd press against her, helpless to stop it, even though he knew she was sleeping and didn't want it. Sometimes his drive was so great he woke her and she turned to him and let him come inside. Years later he felt the coldness in her back, her anger and his hurt and the loneliness in each of them. Then she fell in love with someone else, though he didn't know it, only that he needed to go after her, make her believe in him again.

Now, when he can no longer string sounds into words, when his body is useless, when all sexual desire and function are gone, he reads her love for him in her eyes, feels it in the touch of her hands, the sound of her voice as she reads to him. He is surprised at how busy she keeps herself, how cheerful she is most days—humming or singing as she cooks or does housework, silent only when she reads or writes or works at the computer. Was she always this busy and happy in her daily life? Did the darkness descend only when he was present? She does not hover or interrupt his reverie. After years of simple meals, when she was teaching full-time and writing, she enjoys cooking again. He loves the smells, warmth emanating from the kitchen. She wraps up what's left over and takes it to Joe and Marnie's, freezes it for Cordelia, who visits regularly, gives it to Father O'Neil, the priest from St. Luke's Church in Spooner who comes once a week to give him Communion.

He hears a cupboard in the kitchen opening and closing, a pot knocking against the stove. Soon the room fills with the smell of onions, beef, and vegetables. When the girls were little, he moved their high chairs side by side, pinned bibs around their necks as he fed them creamed carrots from a jar. Their orange faces stare back at him from the window pane. Cordelia chortles and spits carrots back at him. Bea blows hers into bubbles that dribble onto the tray. They laugh as he swipes at their faces with the washcloth.

Hallie pulls up a chair and a small table where she sets a steaming bowl of soup and two cotton towels. One she lays across his upper chest and the other she hangs over her shoulder. She blows on the surface of the soup. He sees the tiny puckers in her lower lip, the downy hair on her skin. When she spills, she lifts the towel from her shoulder and deftly wipes his mouth and chin.

After, she puts on a stack of CDs and bundles up to go out. Each day she walks to the county road, five miles there and back. Unless it's below zero, and then she goes only as far as the red gate. "Need anything?" she calls. Seeing by his face that he's all right, she waves and shuts the door. He hears the crunch of her boots on the path. A wing flickers to his left and a rare chickadee lands on the feeder. *tap tap tap   cheer-up cheerily cheer-up cheerily, what-cheer cheer what-cheer cheer*

The house shifts and groans. Beneath the floor the pine snake sleeps in an S-shaped coil. Eggs lie dormant in the sill between panes of glass. A red squirrel plucks a berry from the hedge and emits a chipping plaint. In Alice's closet her hand-knit sweater slips off a hanger and falls noiselessly to the floor.

A woman appears in the yard, dressed in a brown overcoat. She glides lightly across the snow and disappears into the trees that line the slope above the swamp garden. He watches in his mind's eye as she wends her way along the path. *she knows our voice   many voices not one   she listens   come home Henry come home   she hears the rustling wind   burbling bubbling rising and falling song   trills chirps whistles metallic chips of birds   she slides the pouch with Henry's ashes inside the wall   some of us die before our time   we do not choose   we feel what is lost but it is not grief   we are in we are out of time*

The phone rings and clicks and Cordelia's voice pierces the quiet. "Hi, Dad. I e-mailed you the latest models. The committee liked your triangulated grid and the wrapped walkways. They were especially excited about the idea of drawing water up through the piles and distributing it through the landscape trays. Tell me what you think of the models. I'll be out by dinnertime on Friday. Love you, Dad."

Cordelia is walking toward the house, something held in her cupped hands: eggshells crushed by the bird's weight. Yellowed leaves falling in the spring, acid in the stream, fish filled with toxins. He blinks and she is gone. A movement of white and then another and within minutes the air is filled with snowflakes that blanket the brown grass and melt into the metal-covered stream. He tries to focus on one flake at a time but they are falling too fast and blur into a confetti of white. At his grandfather's window, he knelt as the snow fell on frozen fields. On Christmas Eve, at their home in Minneapolis, he stood on the back deck, meticulously scarring the new-fallen snow. The next morning Beatrice and Cordelia knelt at the dining room window peering out at the perfect line of reindeer tracks. *What do you mean there's no Santa? How the heck did those reindeer tracks get there? Tell me that.* Years later Cordelia found the handmade metal instrument in the garage, the long extender bar, forked ends mimicking the tracks of deer.

He had to wait until the ground had thawed enough to bury his mother. The local cemetery let him keep her in their vault, which was generous since neither she nor his grandfather was buried in that cemetery. The orchard was sacred ground for both of them. Carl dropped two red roses into the newly dug grave, the only black in a field of white.

The snow continues to fall and he hopes that Hallie will turn around and come back. Just the kind of weather they would have snowshoed or hiked in once. In Oslo, he and Sverre Bergström strolled at midnight through the snow, brainstorming ideas for the town hall. In the white he sees a figure. As the form moves closer, he recognizes his father's telltale walk. He wills his hand to move, but the limb lies useless on the sheet. *Where have you been?* Tommy is dressed in the same brown corduroy slacks, navy blue sweater, blue Oxford cloth shirt. His hair and shoulders are flecked with snow.

Tommy stops a few feet from the window and they gaze at one another. Carl has so much he wants to tell him. *I hear things: human voices, living and dead, sounds of the nonhuman world. I hear the creak and groan of the earth, sighs and whistling breaths of hibernating creatures, rasp of roots and silt sifting in the stream. I hear Cordelia and Beatrice at play. I hear my mother, your wife, weeping in the bedroom. I hear music and don't know who is playing— Beatrice or her. I hear Frank Rossi calling me from the street, the click of our sticks against the ball, the El rumbling past my window.*

When Hallie wakes him, he blinks at the darkened meadow, the untouched surface of the snow. She lights the lamps and washes his face and hands. She moves into the kitchen, where he hears her preparations for dinner. Once the casserole is in the oven, she pulls her reading chair close to him, picks up Rilke's *Book of Hours,* and reads:

> *Summer was like your house: you knew*
> *where each thing stood.*
> *Now you must go out into your heart*
> *as onto a vast plain. Now*
> *the immense loneliness begins.*
>
> *The days go numb, the wind*
> *sucks the world from your senses like withered leaves.*

He sees the shadowy trees, tips of wind-burned reeds. Hallie's voice rises and falls like the tumbling stream.

> *Through the empty branches the sky remains.*
> *It is what you have.*
> *Be earth now, and evensong.*
> *Be the ground lying under that sky.*
> *Be modest now, like a thing*
> *ripened until it is real,*
> *so that he who began it all*
> *can feel you when he reaches for you.*

He wants to tell her what it is like to be alive like this. She hides her sadness but he sees the imprint on her face when she returns from her walks. They await Bea's next phone call, Cory's visits, a new chapter of the book she's reading to him, the way the woods change with each passing day. She feeds him, washes him, empties the catheter bag every few hours. It is just the two of them—her voice rising and falling, her hands tending him, her heat beside him.

HALLIE

Chapter 13
Caddis Wood (March)

He sleeps poorly and she, attuned to the sounds he makes when he's in pain or having trouble breathing, is up and down several times a night. Because the hospital bed cannot fit into their small bedroom, she had Joe move their double bed into the shed and replace it with one of the girls' iron beds. At the end of each day, she rolls the hospital bed next to hers so he can sleep beside her. It is like going back in time, only she's listening for *him* now, not the whimper or croupy breathing of a sick child. He can't turn or raise his body to alleviate the painful rigidity in his muscles, can't suction the mucus from his throat or drink from the water glass. She's grown accustomed to it, the way she did when the girls were infants, trying to nap when he does, grateful each time he falls into an unencumbered sleep.

Today, she purees the curried chicken stew she made the night before, a favorite dish of his she hopes will spark his appetite. He tries his best to eat what she feeds him, but she knows he does it for her sake. Who can blame him, having to eat food pureed as if he's an infant? She raises the bed to a sitting position and sits next to him, testing the food with her pinky to make sure it's not too hot. Moving the spoon toward him, she sees the smile in his eyes. *What are you thinking?* she thinks. Talking is such an effort for him now, she doesn't press or question.

As the flesh on his body disappears, his bone structure emerges. There are times when she looks at him and is overwhelmed with grief; at others she is struck dumb by the translucent beauty of his face. His eyes, always one of his best features, grow larger and more expressive by the week. She can read his pain and frustration, his awareness of the steady deterioration in his body. Why did she never read him so clearly before? Was she not looking, not paying attention?

Today he eats more than usual, which makes her happy. She talks to him while she's cleaning up, then shuffles through the books stacked on the floor beside the bed. She reads to him several times a day, choosing what to read depending on his mood. He has asked her to read him her favorites from among the great classics of literature: "I want to have heard them before I die." She's already done *A Portrait of the Artist as a Young Man, Mrs. Dalloway,* and *Heart of Darkness.* When she started reading *Great Expectations,* however, he asked her to stop. "This old stuff isn't doing it for me. Read me something contemporary." So she read him *In Our Time, The Unbearable Lightness of Being,* and short stories by Raymond Carver. He shakes his head when she picks up *Pilgrim at Tinker Creek,* which she started earlier in the week.

"Read . . . from the . . . notebooks," he says hoarsely, moving his chin toward the marble notebooks on her writing table. She takes one and moves the wicker armchair beside him.

August 5, 1928

Another hot night, no relief from the heat. The sun beats on the roof all day so my room is an oven when I go to bed. Last night I snuck down to the back porch and slept on Mormor's old couch. Mama doesn't like it, Lord knows why, so I am back in my room when she comes downstairs to make breakfast. Arthur's with Henry Badenhope at Caddis Wood while I have to work with dumb Alma Lewis in the store. Second summer in a row Arthur and Henry get to work for Mr. Johanssen and I stay home. When it's hot in the woods, the boys just roll out of Henry's front door and into the swimming hole. Mama says she wouldn't want the Badenhopes' cabin by the swimming hole because it is so noisy but I think it's the best location in Caddis Wood. Mama took pity on me yesterday and let me go to the lake with Liska and Ruthie Dickinson.

Today I'm scooping sticky prunes and apricots into brown paper sacks: 2 pounds of prunes, 17 cents; 1 pound of apricots, 10 cents. I told Mama it's stupid to have me bagging prunes while Alma, who's got oatmeal for brains, is in charge of dry goods. "She's seventeen years old, Alice," Mama says. "So what!" I say back. "She has no sense of color or style, and her stitches aren't as straight as mine." Mama gives me the evil eye so I keep quiet.

I can't wait until Labor Day. Papa will close the store and we'll be in the woods the whole week. Mama will have a fit if she sees me jumping off the rope swing. I'm the best jumper because I weigh the least. I know it burns Henry, who doesn't like to lose, especially to a girl. It doesn't matter how often he tries—no way can he or Arthur catch me.

"More?" she asks.

"Read . . . when . . . Will goes off . . . to Korea."

She goes into the bedroom to find the right notebook and takes her seat again on the wicker chair.

October 4, 1950

Will's in the First Marine Division. We listen to the news every day, pray there's no telegram or visit from a Marine chaplain.

If I see one coming, I'm closing the curtains and locking the door. Stu MacFadden and another boy from Westside High are already dead. Will said he trusts General MacArthur but what does that mean? If Will's division is outnumbered by North Korean and Chinese soldiers, what good is MacArthur to them? I framed Will's photograph in his dress blues. He's so handsome. He looks more like a man now than a boy. I get down on my knees every night and pray for his safety. Please, God, let this war END.

November 28, 1950

Henry answered the door before I could stop him. I saw the man's uniform through the glass. Henry's shoulders sagged and I heard the awful sound he made. Will died two days ago in the battle at Changjin Reservoir in North Korea. The First Marine Division was badly outnumbered by Chinese forces. Henry has flown to Washington to pick up Will's body. I feel a coward for not going with him. You can cry until you're wrung inside out but it does no good. Nothing prepares you for this kind of grief. Maureen MacFadden came over to sit with me. She said it will get easier but one look in her eyes and you know it's not true.

August 26, 1951

I told Henry this would be the day but now that it's here I can't bear to think of letting go of him. But we promised each other we would lay him to rest before the end of the summer. I took out the black velvet pouch and opened it, letting the light fall on Will's ashes. How do you outlive your child and still find happiness in the world? Henry wants to put Will's Purple Heart with the pouch so I will wrap them both in plastic and lay them inside Mama's silver box. We will open the wall and put the box next to Mama and Papa's ashes. Then it will be over. Part of him is scattered over Echo Pond and the rest is here in Papa's wall.

"My . . . ashes," he says.

"I know, honey."

"No . . . way to l—i—v—e." He draws out the last word, can barely get the *v* sound out.

Her eyes fill and she strokes his face with her hand. He closes his eyes. She lowers the hospital bed so he's in a semireclining position. Any flatter and the secretions will build up in his throat and disrupt his breathing. When she knows he's asleep, she calls the Pratts, and Marnie promises to come right over. Marnie and Joe take turns relieving her in the afternoons so she can get out. She's afraid to leave him alone now, so the only break in the day is her daily walk or run into town for groceries. Carl is happy when he wakes up to find Joe there, for Joe talks about his latest construction projects.

She adjusts the blind so the sunlight isn't too strong on his face. His body is so small now in the bed—day by day he shrinks. Although he gets testy when he's in pain or out of patience with the awful, trapped nature of his condition, his grace in the face of it puts her to shame. As hard as it is for her, what must it be like for him?

When she hears Marnie's boots on the walk, she swings the door open.

"Brought you the mail," Marnie says brightly, her cheeks red from the cold.

Hallie turns off the lane and hikes through unbroken snow to the fishpond. The snow is knee deep and she can feel the sweat beneath her down jacket by the time she reaches Sand Creek. She crosses the bridge and turns north along what is in summer a well-tended path. Tall maize-colored grasses creak in the wind and she touches her mittens to their ruddy, stiffened tips. At the curve in the stream, she looks upstream to where the beavers built a dam almost thirty years ago, creating a small pool where Henry Badenhope fell through. The water is running clear and cold; she cannot remember ever seeing ice there.

The wind chips at her face and she shivers thinking of Henry trying to make his way home in the subzero cold. What must it have been like for Alice to find him frozen in the snow?

"Why did this happen to us?" She is surprised at the sound of her voice in the silent air. "I want him back the way he was. I want our old life back, not this stupid-ass new one we're living."

She swipes at her face, hating the ever-present tears, and plows up the hill toward McGaugheys' cabin. Her weeping merges with the clack of dry seed pods, whistling reeds, Livy's tinkling wind chimes. She hates it when she lets her grief get the better of her. She needs these walks for renewal, for the cushion necessary to get her through the day.

Halfway up the hill she regrets having left the road. She's out of breath and her back and legs ache from maneuvering through thick snow. When she reaches McGaugheys' back deck, she sits on the edge and flops backward on the wood, flinging wide her arms. Gazing up, she studies the pearl-gray sky through the blurred lace of her eyelashes.

A shout startles her and she pulls herself up in time to see a flash of red and yellow through the open kitchen door and Livy— *Livy!*—racing toward her. She catches her as Livy drops to her knees on the deck. After a long minute rocking back and forth, they pull back and gaze at each other. Grief and age have etched new lines in Livy's face, thinner and tauter than before, ashen hair streaked with white. Her eyes, however, are once again the beautiful sea green Hallie remembers. Gone is the dull, splotchy film that covered them after Tim died, the haunted way they swerved and skittered each time the two women met.

Hallie's heart races. "When did you get here—I thought you were staying in India until spring—how long are you here? Are you . . ."

"Come in," Livy says, helping Hallie to her feet. "We'll have tea. Lucas is on his way over to your house."

As she enters the bright, familiar room, Hallie is overcome with emotion. She bows her head, annoyed at the ever-ready rush of tears.

"It's okay, Hal." Livy pours hot water into a teapot and sets the pot and cups on the table. "Take your coat off. Sit."

When they're seated across from each other, Livy reaches across the table and covers Hallie's cold hands with her own. "I'm sorry we didn't come sooner."

"It doesn't . . ."

"Yes, it does. We should have come. But we're here now. Lucas plans to rejoin his practice, though only part-time. I'm going to rent a studio in Minneapolis—I've been painting like a madwoman. Wait until you see."

"I can't wait to see your paintings, Liv."

"Is Cordelia all right?"

"Yes. You know she's moved to Wisconsin and is working on the project with Carl's firm."

Livy nods.

"She's here every weekend. I don't know what I'd do without her. She's going to be so happy to see you."

"And Bea—the pregnancy is going all right?"

"So far, so good. She can't travel, though, so she's not able to see Carl, which is very hard on her. I hoped he'd hang on until the baby comes, but I don't think he's going to make it. Things are deteriorating very fast."

"I'm so sorry, Hal."

"I'm just so glad to see you. There's . . ." She hesitates.

"What?"

She shakes her head. "There's no one to talk about this with. But you . . . God, Liv, you don't need this."

"Hallie, I know what you're going through."

"It's hard."

"Tell me."

She talks fast, weeping uncontrollably. The list of losses is so long and she hates the sound of her voice speaking them. But all of it is true. She longs to be touched, to make love, to hear the sound of his voice talking to her the way he used to. She wants to sit across from him while he eats, to hike the paths with him, pick raspberries at the berry farm, talk to him about the girls.

"I'm so afraid, Livy. Afraid that I'm never going to see him again, that I'll die without ever feeling real pleasure or happiness again."

Livy is leaning forward, her face close to Hallie's. "Not seeing him again—it breaks your heart in two. But you *will* feel happiness again. The light will come back eventually—it can't help itself. Nature can't tolerate a vacuum."

She stands up, lifts the kettle off the stove, and refills the teapot. "I'm such a sage now. Slap me when I'm too obnoxious."

Hallie laughs and takes the Kleenex Livy hands her.

"If you're up for going out again, I'd like to see him," Livy says.

"Yes," Hallie says, rising.

CARL

Chapter 14

Caddis Wood (May)

Flashes of gold spangle the dark. Garlic wafts from the red-and-white mottled spathe of a skunk cabbage. Green shoots erupt from damp soil, burst of green-and-white trillium against brown.

"Look, Daddy, look!" Cordelia calls from the bridge. She and Bea sit side by side, bare feet dangling a few inches above the water. Their popsicle-stick boat gets caught and taken by the current.

"Here, Daddy, we're just going to roll you over." Cordelia supports his shoulder as she and Hallie turn him onto his side. He shudders at the putrid smell—*turn your face, don't look*—naked as a baby in an old man's waste, so much fluid, his body rocking in its own sea. They busy themselves with the sheet. Hallie cleans him and they slide on a new pair of pajama bottoms. His throat hurts from the feeding tube. He tries to signal Hallie with his eyes: *Stop feeding me. It is hideous and will only prolong things.* There is no dignity to dying. His head shakes with tremors, he chokes on his own saliva, food goes right through. His feet are cold and nothing they do warms them.

Hallie rubs Vaseline on his lips. Blue eyes through fog. The fog lifts him off the bed and carries him into the woods. It hovers a few feet above the grass in Osprey Meadow, caressing it like a lover. The girls hold lightly to his jacket, one on either side of him. Bea has been limping heavily since the fork in the logging road. A sudden, frenzied *cheereek!* as the osprey lifts off the blackened trunk. Bea puts both hands to her face, overcome with emotion.

The fog thickens—white, everywhere he looks. He calls out for the girls but his voice is weak and far away and then it is gone and all he can hear is wind. He recognizes the doctor's voice and wants to shout: *Take this tube out. Do not put anything else in my body.* Another voice. He blinks and it is Lucas leaning over him. Then the black coat and white collar and Father O'Neil's sad eyes through white. He is laying out things on the table beside the bed—oil, prayer book—the tools of sacrament. *Hail Mary, full of Grace, the Lord is with thee. Blessed art thou among women, and blessed is the fruit of thy womb, Jesus.* Cold inches up his legs—it is past his knees. Why won't anyone put another blanket on him, all the blankets in the house, his legs like ice?

The fog fingers his neck—the mist clears suddenly, sun beaming through, and he sees the blue Oxford shirt and nut-brown hair and his father's face above the bed. The fog lifts him again, heavy like smoke, and they are in Tommy Fens's office, sitting on the high swivel chairs at the drafting table. He smells the sweet tobacco smoke on his father's fingers, watches the swift, assured strokes of his father's pencil on tracing paper.

Father O'Neil's voice murmurs and sings, and the man's thumb is on his forehead. The priest is anointing other parts of his body but he can't feel anything but the cold. His mother is white and cold in the orchard ground. Tim McGaughey is in the ground, too, but he is not cold because he was burned. His father was burned also, only a charred skeleton in the coffin, but he walks the earth again. Can he feel the cold, the heat?

He didn't want to touch the ashes in the shoebox, the singed blue ribbon. "I burned the letters," Hallie said, laying the box in his lap. "I shouldn't have saved them. I love *you*. I'm sorry. Forgive me. Please, honey, forgive me."

It is so hard to breathe—horrible, shrill rasp.

"I'm here, Dad." Cordelia takes his hand in hers.

He shakes his head, or thinks he does, and Hallie brushes his cheek with her lips. "I'm here, honey. We're both here."

"We love you, Dad."

It is his own breathing making that sound. *I'm ready, Lord.* He stands in the snow at his mother's grave and thinks of his grandfather waiting for her. Rosary beads click against the pews. She is inside the oak casket being lowered into the earth. Hallie will scatter his ashes on Echo Pond. He wants Hallie to read Rilke to him but of course he can't tell her, so he says the words aloud in his head.

God, give us each our own death,
the dying that proceeds
from each of our lives:

the way we loved,
the meanings we made,
our need.

He drifts and turns like a leaf on the stream, cold water soaking his groin. Beneath the surface animals are feeding, mating, laying eggs. Leeches loop through leaves looking for food. Frogs eat water beetles. Beetles feed on tadpoles. Tadpoles eat water fleas. Mayfly nymphs sprout wings. The industry is dizzying and he rises through thick, spreading stems into yellow air. Pollen sprung from male catkins, from the heads of pond sedge.

Whoosh of wind, a shadow on the stream, blue wings edged in black.

The room is darker now, the voices cars rushing on a highway late at night. Cold blankets his chest. His back, his chest, his bones ache. Grandpa Fens is a big, skinny bird with a bald head, hunched back, hands tight on the black-tipped cane. "Pull my pinky," he says to the boy. "Go ahead, don't be afraid." The fingers are gnarled and bent, the hand a claw, hardly human. Carl doesn't want to, but the old man insists. His brown eyes are wet with glee.

As Carl pulls the hobbled finger, the old man leans his head back in a kind of ecstasy, then cries out in pain. "Stop that!" his father scolds. "You're hurting him." He tries to shift position in the bed. Why won't someone move him? He longs for heat, for summer. On the beach in Captiva, he lay on the blanket with Hallie bathed in sunlight. The long stretch of sand, horizon line halving sky and sea. A shadow falls over his face and he rises to his elbow as the bird lands inches away. He swallows, mesmerized by the fluttering feathers and graceful head. The bird's eyes are black, ringed with yellow. It stands motionless: three, four, five minutes. Then, as the air blows and cools, the long neck contracts into an S. He is barely breathing as the lozenge of light shrinks and the neck folds into itself and disappears, body and neck joined at the shoulders.

"Daddy? It's Bea. Jack's here, too. Can you hear me, Dad?" Bea's voice quivers with tears. "I love you so much, Daddy." Her voice breaks and Jack's voice is on the line but he can't hear the words. The phone is in Hallie's hands, blue eyes through fog. Frost in his ears and his chest reaches for air. Acrid, rotting vegetables, dead things in the room. Cordelia rubs lotion on his hands. He sees her briefly, as the mist clears, dark foam blooming on the surface of the stream, new winged flies rising into silver air. One day, two if they're lucky, as they mate, lay their eggs, die together on the moving stream. The room darkens.

He tastes salt, feels death in the tumbling waves. His mother sweeps him up in her arms and carries him onto the beach. Her heart beats beneath his cheek. He burrows into her arms, not wanting to be put down or enter the ocean again. Hallie calls him to join her in the water. She presses her body against him and he wraps his arms around her, feeling her pelvic bones, soft breasts, salt on her lips and tongue. It is the end of the day, nearing sunset. He still reels at the newness of their passion, the sorrow of the past months and year. *You're my family,* he says to her, straining to see. Cold as ice. His head presses back into the pillow as he labors to breathe.

A sunbeam pours through the unglazed oculus and bathes the concrete coffers in the dome of the Pantheon. Concrete mixed with pumice. At the bottom of the dome the concrete is heavy and thick but lighter at the top. He charts the passing day through the shadows on the granite floor and the Great Eye gazing down at him. In the Piazza della Rotonda he sits on the bench near the fountain and makes sketch after sketch of the portico.

"I love you," Hallie says softly in his ear. Her warm hands on his face. "I've always loved you, Carl, *always.*"

His father takes one hand as they walk toward the waves—his mother takes the other. The black underbellies of the waves smell of dead fish with open mouths and teeth. His father smiles and squeezes his hand. The girls hold tightly to his jacket as he puts the flashlight into his pocket. "There's nothing to be afraid of," he says to them. "Let your eyes grow accustomed to the dark. The moon and stars will guide us." They gaze into the ghostly night and wait for the trees to take shape.

The moon grows lighter as they walk. Light and dark and light and dark. Cicadas scream in his ears. Nan and Tommy are standing by the shed as he and the girls cross the lawn. Hallie waits at the door. The light shines on her hair and she is smiling. The air is thick with cottonwood, thick clusters of crab apples, Henry's fluttering moths. Tim casts—once, twice—the line loops and arcs, falling perfectly on the surface of the stream. He is standing knee deep in the stream, his strong feet and legs anchoring him in the current, his young face and hands pinking in the sun.

The crane's neck languidly unfurls and stretches up and out toward the water. The burnished disk inches toward a milky sea. The sun is a deep berry red. Pearly waves break on the polished sand. His neck strains and reaches—for air, for light—as dark fills the room. The sun touches the sea and floods the sky with color. He puts his arm around Hallie and draws her closer. *I am here with you watching, nothing past or present, only this moment this beach this sun. Now.* They do not speak as the scarlet disk changes shape, transforms the horizon. A sliver left, the sky in flames.

"Take my hand, son." The boy squeezes hard and the three of them run toward the water. The sun winks once and is gone, only the vermilion sky, the waves, the lilting stream, the wind.

Chapter 15

Caddis Wood (August)

Hallie sets the empty glass in the sink and takes her wide-brimmed straw hat from the table. After checking to make sure that the small lacquered box is tucked securely inside her backpack, she slips in the envelope full of photographs.

The lane is a luminous gold ribbon through corridors of green. Not as hot as last Sunday when she and Cordelia hiked to the swimming hole. Such a day, the Clam moving languidly, sun sizzling on the bank, the Morans' house closed up tight so no chance of anyone watching. Cordelia pulled two black inner tubes from the post in the Morans' backyard and tied them together. After the first shock of spring-fed water, they waded upstream to the bridge, where Hallie looped the rope round the bridge post and they floated side by side, bobbing like two corks.

Parallel lines of laundry hang behind the Pratts' house. Marnie sees her from the window and waves. Hallie is grateful for her and Joe's many kindnesses, for the goodwill of all her neighbors here. As the road rises and curves past the turnoff to McGaugheys', her heart lifts. For the past two days she and Livy have been transplanting maidenhair ferns from the shady copse along Raven's Ridge to the new-turned earth beneath McGaugheys' deck. This morning Livy drove home to Minneapolis to get her studio ready for the weekend art crawl. Only one week to the grand opening of the Upper Mississippi River Park and Research Center, when they all will be together again, including Beatrice and Jack and three-year-old Will.

Her feet sink into the mossy floor of the pine grove, dark and silent as a chapel. Livy's red ribbons still mark the path into the woods, recently mowed and trimmed. The industrious Moran boys, teenagers now, have become keepers of the trails. She fingers the black box beneath the canvas.

At the top of the hill overlooking Echo Pond, she gazes gratefully at the incandescent surface. Another week and the feathery larches will start to yellow, but not yet. Trees cast their shadows on the stippled surface. Water striders and whirligig beetles zigzag merrily. No otters anywhere. Hallie makes her way down the hill to the rowboat, banked on its side under a red pine. A few weeks ago she hiked here, checked for leaks, paid Jimmy Moran to paint it and repair the oarlocks.

She nods in approval at the boy's workmanship and shoves the boat to the water's edge. She puts her day pack inside and pushes off. The oars fit easily into the locks; the steady lift and pull work the muscles in her back and shoulders, sore from the week's transplanting. Where sunlight strikes, the water is molten silver, turning to bronze near shore. She shields her eyes as a flock of swallows wheels overhead. When she reaches the middle, she puts up the oars and drifts.

Taking the lacquered box and envelope out of the pack, she places them lightly on her lap. Her hands are a mess: veins visible through loose skin dotted with age spots, nails broken and inlaid with garden dirt. She sighs. For three years she's thought about this day.

She takes out the photos of Will—right after birth, and at

intervals of weeks and months up to his third birthday in June—
and lays them on the seat. She wishes Carl could see him: he has
Jack's sturdy frame and cleft chin, Bea's gentian-blue eyes and
russet hair—the black having fallen out a few weeks after his
birth. One month after Carl died she flew to Seattle for Will's
birth. She was happy with the name—*William Carl*—calling
him Will the first time she held him, stunned at his shock of
black hair. Even though he was two weeks early, he weighed a
solid seven pounds eight ounces, and had a loud, lusty cry.

"There is so much to tell you," she says softly. "He's more active than Bea was as a baby, more like Cordelia, or Jack maybe.
He walked at eleven months, doesn't nap until he's exhausted
himself—then he crashes. Poor Bea. But he's musical—we know
that. Bea plays CDs all day and he hums along, plays a kazoo
Clare bought him."

She wants him to know that her debilitating sorrow has ebbed
and there are days now when she is almost happy. She's writing again, poem after poem. "Cordelia and I have taken down
the fence around the vegetable garden. It's too much work. Joe
is getting older and the Moran boys are so busy. Besides, I enjoy
going to the farmers' market or the co-op. I'm sorry if I'm letting
you down. You were the true grower in the family, not me. You
won't believe how many animals have come in to feast on the remains. The red fox family have made a den!

"I told Cordelia and Beatrice how we wanted things divided.
They're fine with everything."

Deep in the winter before he died, they rewrote the will. He
thought very carefully about which of his things he wanted each
of them to have. After Hallie's death, the family assets would be
divided evenly between the girls. He wanted it clear that Beatrice
and her family would always be welcome at Caddis Wood, but

the deed would pass to Cordelia. "It is yours in spirit," he wrote to her, "yours to enjoy and shepherd into the future."

"If there's truly a heaven, I hope you're there. I hope you can rest knowing we're all right. I'm sorry I didn't do this earlier—I meant to, but I just couldn't let go."

She hugs the box to her, feeling the boat's slow drift. Then she lifts the lid, shields the contents with her hand so the wind won't stir it before she's ready, and lovingly fingers the tiny bits of bone. Earlier that morning she took a teaspoonful and put it in a velvet pouch she'd made for that purpose. The next time Cordelia visits, they will bury it in the wall alongside Alice's, Henry's, and Will's ashes. But this day, this good-bye, belongs to her.

She gazes round once more at the woven shadows of green and brown along the shore. Tipping the contents into her hand, she waits for the breeze. When it comes, a sweep of swallows with it, she opens her hand and flings wide the ash and bone. All the days of her married life fly with him into the blue air, motes suspended in sunlight, and then in a sleeve of wind he is gone.

At breakfast Jack reads aloud from the Sunday *Star Tribune* Arts & Entertainment section, whose front page is devoted to the new park and research center. Hallie places cut-up pieces of peach in front of Will and licks the sweet pulp from her fingers. The article gives a brief history of the site, a summary of the reclamation strategies undertaken to remediate the landscape, and a positive review of the overall design of the research center itself.

"He actually mentions Dad's triangulated grid," Cordelia says happily, taking the paper from Jack.

Hallie smiles and places a B-shaped pancake on Bea's plate. "Eat."

"Oh, Mom, I'm full."

Hallie knocks Jack's arm with the spatula as he tries to sneak the pancake off Bea's plate. "Not you. *Her.*"

Bea gives Hallie an exasperated look and puts a bite of pancake in her mouth. "I'm eating enough—*honest.* Ever since Will was born, my metabolism is in overdrive."

Cordelia, still flipping through the paper, calls out. "Mom, there's a review of your book!"

"Let me see." Hallie reaches for the paper but Cordelia dodges her.

"It's good, Mom, really."

Hallie plucks the paper from Cordelia's hands. "I'm going to read this upstairs, in private."

"Well, my metabolism could use a kick so I'm going for a run. Want to join me?" Cordelia looks tellingly at Jack, who's just finished off Bea's pancake. "Sure," he says with a grin. "You mind?" to Bea, who lifts Will off the booster seat and waves him off. "Go. Clare and Nathan will be here soon, so Will and I will have lots of playmates."

Hallie leaves Bea and Will to the half-built Lego tower in the living room and climbs the stairs with newspaper in hand. Once she's inside the bedroom, curled comfortably on her bed, she reads the review. She nods, satisfied, and leans back against the headboard. Much as she loves having them all here, she is no longer used to so much activity in the house and looks for opportunities to sneak away to the solitude of her own room. Who would have thought that she, who so loved living in the nucleus of a family, would grow to like living alone? She lifts the new book from her bedside table and runs her hands over the cover.

The day sprints forward. Midafternoon, Will crashes, which is a blessing, Bea says, or he'd never make it through the evening. At five, after everyone has showered and dressed, and Lucas and

Livy have arrived, Hallie opens a bottle of champagne and they toast Fens and Thorne, Cordelia and her team. For the next hour they drink champagne and finish off Hallie's hors d'oeuvres.

"We should go," Hallie says finally, picking up Will.

She and Cordelia park at the entry point south of the building so they can approach it from the meadow. The wooden walkway hovers a foot above grade, brushed by plumes of native prairie grass that spill away in all directions. The heat of the day is gone and there is a cooling breeze. In the distance the glass research center winks in the waning sunlight. As they walk, Cordelia explains to the group how they rerouted and stabilized the shoreline of Battle Creek, filled in some of the ponds to slow the migration of contaminants, and added organic rich soil to prevent erosion.

When they enter the dappled light within one of the wrapped walkways, Cordelia pulls Will out of the stroller and holds him up to an opening in the triangulated metal grid. She beams when he spies the underwater plants, their squiggly, waving roots beneath the trays.

"Which ones are these?" Livy asks.

"Water lettuce, giant duckweed, and water fern," Cordelia says. Hallie's eyes brim. "It's hard to believe, isn't it?"

"Yes, Mama, it is."

As they near the building, the lowering sun catches the glass and exposed metal and sets them afire. The formal copse of birch trees, pruned so that the leafy branches begin at the base of the building, creates a golden haze on either side of the saffron cube. People, visible through translucent floors, ripple and blur like figures in a dream. Before they ascend, Cordelia walks them round the "Healing Ground" she began early on in the process, her first experiment with the hyperaccumulator plants, and along a path that bisects the shade garden beneath the building.

Exiting the elevator, they enter a space awash in light and color, muted tones of furniture and floor coverings creating a neutral ground for the bright clothing worn by the people at the opening. Already the room is buzzing with voices and activity, and the elevator doors open and close, bringing more people in. Hallie greets Alex, colleagues of his and Carl's, friends from the university, neighbors.

There are speeches, welcomes and accolades from the mayor and officials from the Minnesota Pollution Control Agency and the Upper Mississippi River Research Council, and then a short film showing the evolution of the project. Hallie smiles as Cordelia appears, talking about the role of plants and trees. Her breath catches when Carl's face floods the screen. She is aware of Livy on one side of her and Bea on the other but it is as if she is encased in glass, all sound and sensation muted except for the face on the screen, thin but full of life and color, brown eyes aglow.

As the film ticks on, she half hears bits and pieces of the narration: photovoltaic panels, movable wall panels, recycled water, cutouts through the building that let in light. A disquieting feeling of déjà vu settles over her and she remembers the opening at the Weisman five years ago. Little did any of them know that festive night what lay ahead. Not death, not this building, not this ruined landscape now under renewal.

Although she continues to greet and talk with people, she maintains a strange sense of remove from it all. She yearns for a quiet room to sit in and gather her thoughts, process the whirlwind of feelings and memories roiling through her. She searches for Bea and Jack and Will, hoping they're looking for an excuse to go home, but when she finds them, Will is sleeping peacefully in the stroller and Bea is talking animatedly with Livy and Lucas. Hallie moves to one of the large exterior glass windows and gazes out at the slow-falling dusk. She slips through an exit door and descends to the ground floor and goes outside.

Slowly, happily, she follows the wooden walkway across the replanted prairie toward distant poplar groves. Swales of new vegetation thicken the edge of Battle Creek Lake, tinged violet by the dying sun. A sleepy cicada buzzes in the grass, not yet awake. Reaching the first fork where the paths split south and east, she turns to face the research center, leaning her lower back against the railing. The sun has set but the afterglow remains, burnishing the glass and casting a tawny light through freckled trees. Roused, cicadas click and hum, joined now by crickets and frogs.

Lights inside the building flicker, flooding the ground beneath. *A tiny hearth amidst the trees,* she thinks. People within are a tableau of moving silhouettes. She remembers that night in Cornwall, Carl's shadow looming over hers as they walked onto the empty beach. In the orange glow thrown by the chapel on the mount, their oversized heads and arms resembled cutout paper dolls. She was twenty-three years old, he twenty-six.

Memories like these once filled her with despair. After Carl died, there was no bottom to her loneliness. Now, scenes from the past create an island in her mind, not unlike what happens when she turns off the county road and enters the green light of Caddis Wood. *Green time,* Carl used to say, trying to put words to the way in which time shifted shape inside the forest. She is not a religious person like Carl, but she feels the spirit in the woods, the way she feels it here.

In the purple dusk, blood-tipped bluestem vibrate with electric song. Leaning over the railing, she studies the full seed heads shaped like turkeys' feet, struck by the paradox of this field of new, healthy prairie rooted in poison. Despite the remediation going on all around her, parts of the park are too contaminated to fix. Capped with new soils, they must remain fenced to protect the public. The restoration of the rest, for all the progress made, is still experimental.

She rests her hand on the sun-warmed wood of the railing and listens. So much sound in the swelling grass. Sometimes the sound changes, carries an echo of something else she can't put words to—a *voice* she tried to re-create in her last book, infusing its cadence into the poems. She hears it building behind the shushing wind, the honk of migrating geese, the buzzing thrumming clicking drone of insects.

"Mama!"

Cordelia is waving to her from the end of the walkway. Her silk dress swings as she walks, shimmering in the glow cast by the building's exterior lights. Far off an egret emits a loud, guttural croak followed by a series of high-pitched, laughing chips. As Hallie moves toward her, she scans the dusky lip of Battle Creek Lake. Cordelia reaches her and they stand arm in arm, looking for the bird. "There!" Cordelia cries, pointing to the white speck in the distance, his head turned toward the luminous research center floating like a harvest moon among the trees.

Acknowledgments

This novel took a long time to write, so there are many people to thank. To all those who acted as readers, guides, and sources of support during the writing of this novel, including the wonderful writers and students at Hamline, the poets I know who helped me to inhabit the interior life of Hallie Fens, and the amazing WWWs, I thank you. A huge thanks to Graywolf Press for its long support of my work as a writer, to its hardworking and gifted staff, and particularly to Fiona McCrae for her careful editing and to Katie Dublinski for making the process seem so seamless. I am grateful to my dear friends who gave me such sound revision advice—Sheila O'Connor, Alison McGhee, Patricia Straub, Mary Logue, Julie Schumacher, and Kate DiCamillo. Thank you, Gail See, for believing in this novel and sharing my love for its setting. Thank you to Andy and Pepper Fuller, Lee Hoteling, and Julie Bargmann for their knowledge of landscape and forestry. To my daughters and husband—Maura, Siobhan, and Garth Rockcastle—I owe my respect for the value and beauty of good architecture and sustainable design, my interest in the restoration of the Pig's Eye dump, and my ability to write about it. Heartfelt thanks to Regan Golden for the inspired artwork that graces the cover. My love and deep appreciation to Deborah Keenan and Pat Francisco, faithful friends and insightful readers who were with me from the beginning. *In Caddis Wood* is dedicated to my husband, Garth Rockcastle, who shares my love for this landscape, whose partnership in a long-ago project inspired the book, and who sustained me throughout.

MARY FRANÇOIS ROCKCASTLE is the author of *Rainy Lake*. She is the director of The Creative Writing Programs at Hamline University, and the founding and executive editor of *Water~Stone Review*. She lives in Minneapolis.

Book design by Rachel Holscher.
Composition by BookMobile Design and
Publishing Services, Minneapolis, Minnesota.
Manufactured by Versa Press on acid-free
30 percent postconsumer wastepaper.